"1968"

By
William Natale

Based on a story by William Natale & Roland Ghetty

Image Workshop Press

Dedication

To my parents who taught me to reach for the stars and to my children who keep me grounded.

Acknowledgements

Thanks to the many who helped me on the journey to completing this book, including Jim Riordan, Roland Ghetty, Chuck Stepner, Bill Messner, Juan Ramirez, Myki Romano, Renee and Gina Natale.

Disclaimer

This book is entirely fiction. Any similarity to real individuals is entirely coincidental.

ISBN – 978-0-692-40696-0

Pau3-026-589 - copyright
Registered, WGAw #1095750

I am an ordinary man and always will remain as such, but the life I've lived is without question extraordinary for having experienced the times and tribulations of 1968.

CHAPTER ONE

THE INVITATION

"Is that not the most perfect line to open a story? That's why it's a classic." Brother Joel, a short balding man with the look of Friar Tuck, smiled at the twelve seniors, disciples of his advanced English course, the cream of St. Patrick's class of 1968 on Chicago's all-white northwest side. Joel pursued the point as he held up a copy of his tattered *A Tale of Two Cities* before his charges that sat in a circle before him in a room unlike any other in the school. Joel reclined in a leather armchair before a wall of dark oak shelves filled with leather bound novels. The shelves wrapped around the two other interior walls. Decorative gold lamps with beige lampshades illuminated the room giving it the feel of a Tudor study. The boys each had an English high back Tudor chair with a small iron wrought glass table next to it for books and writing notes.

"Do any of you think that's true of the time you live in?" The avuncular Brother turned to his right to gaze through a wall of glass that looked onto a corridor filled with spring rain. He waited. Finally a hand went up. Joel nodded.

"It's only April fourth and already we've had one of our naval ships commandeered by the North Koreans, LBJ announcing he won't run again for election, the Tet offensive in Vietnam that's convinced many that this war is not winnable, a draft that casts a shadow over the lives of me, my brother and my friends and our quest to get into the college of our choice, not to mention the test."

"Without question Joseph, an accurate depiction of life today, but does the test deserve to be with the rest?"

Joe Beriso appreciated the irony of his mentor's inquiry since it had been preceded with the notion that his comment was "without question." Joe hated the exactness that Brother Joel demanded; it made him reticent to participate in class, however, he had to admit that he had allowed emotion to obscure his judgment to deliver a concise answer. Passing the dreaded AP (a-k-a "advanced placement test"), secured for those high school seniors who succeeded, a year of English college credit. The AP, a mere month away served as a barometer of excellence that verified and, some say vindicated, Brother Joel's prestigious program and his selection of apostles.

Beriso held a rank of 44 out of 448 students; he was within the top ten percent but that paled in comparison with his classmates who held the top thirteen positions of the class of 1968. Joe was the last student of fourteen selected for Honors English. Many of his colleagues were convinced that Joe got the final spot in deference to his older brother Vince, a tall, athletic, attractive Brother Joel-favorite and 1967 valedictorian.

Vince chastised Joe, usually at dinner in front of their parents, to work extra hard so as "not to shame the Beriso name." Whenever that happened, mother Gloria, immediately came to the defense of her baby. "Vince, your brother will do just fine when his time comes to take that test." Father John didn't dare say a word against his wife's admonition, but shot Joe a look that read, "Heed your brother's advice - don't screw it up."

The previous May, Vince had scored a 3.0 out of a possible five points. A 3.0 was considered average, but more importantly, the minimum score required to pass. Only two students in the history of Brother Joel's class had scored a 4.0 and no one had ever achieved the unthinkable, the unattainable 5.0.

Vince complained that the AP was the hardest, toughest and most grueling of all the standardized national tests that he had ever taken. The pressure to perform weighed on Joe's mind much the same way that the albatross hung around the neck of Samuel Taylor Coleridge's *Ancient Mariner*. The visual was a bit over the top but apparently apropos for advanced Honors English students.

"You're right," said Joe. "The test doesn't belong in that construction. Come to think of it, neither does college."

"Very good!" Brother Joel paused, using the silence like a gifted composer to set up his next note of advice. "Remember gentleman when you write your essays for the AP test, less is more."

* * *

A smoky haze permeated the skies above as a lean, middle-aged, executively dressed Dane Anderson ambled up the front apron of a proscenium-arched brownstone. At the top of the arch etched in stone were the words, "ANDERSON INC. FLUID DISTRIBUTORS." Dane entered his factory passing through stylish open bi-fold doors that had been hand crafted to fit the curve of the arch. The doors had small rectangular windows at the top. Dane carried a small white paper sandwich bag.

From six production lines, three on the left and three on the right of a roadway marked with yellow capped letters,

FORKLIFT PATHWAY, Anderson Inc. dispensed a myriad of automotive chemicals, lighter fluids, oils, kerosene and turpentine from overhead vats. Anderson filled canisters of all shapes and sizes moving on conveyor belts. The plant employed fifty workers to operate the machinery, package, warehouse, and ship the products to major department and hardware stores in Chicago and across the country. All the workers were black with the exception of Dane's secretary, a light skinned mulatto of Negro and French ancestry and Diego, a Cuban refugee who worked as the plant janitor.

Anderson, a small but vital firm fit nicely with City Hall's plan to foster local job development in Chicago's neighborhoods. The word "neighborhood" was code. Whites heard "neighborhood" and felt safe. In their lexicon it meant boundaries that protect and more importantly separate and exclude.

Blacks heard "neighborhood" as code for an urban community where institutions, churches and social support organizations made life tolerable for denizens of ghetto housing.

Chicago proudly pointed at the newly created constructed housing campuses, dubbed by the press as "projects," as affordable shelter for the indigent who came from the South to work in its factories. It was the educated Negro leaders, perceived by white power brokers as trouble makers, who saw the projects for what they were...segregated islands isolated inconspicuously by insidious inner city planning that included construction of man-made ten lane expressway barriers, ironically hailed by that same Chicago press, critical of the projects, as modern marvels.

The aroma, wafting from the bag Dane carried, drew sniffs and longing looks from employees on the lines. The scent was obvious, a sandwich exquisitely prepared by "Jimmy & Gina's Italian Beef and Cuisine." The restaurant take-out joint located under a railroad viaduct a mere block away served mouth watering food. Until recently it had been a favorite with Anderson employees. "Jimmy & Gina's" was so close yet so far away ever since *The Watchdogs*, a gang of Italian thugs, claimed the eatery to be exclusively in white territory. Their leader, Dominick, brazenly spray painted, graffiti style, the viaduct's bulwark with the words, "Niggers Keep Out." It was a line in the sand that no Negro dare cross.

Dane climbed a black iron stairway to an office suite built using an actual Pullman train car. It hung from the ceiling in the center of the plant. From windows on either side of the Pullman with electric blinds that opened in an instant, Dane could track the activity of his plant, warehouse and shipping areas.

Prior to the retirement of Frank Sullivan, a foreman with twenty years of experience, Dane enjoyed the luxury of only having to concentrate on the business of the front office. With the promotion of Clarence Wilson, from a production line operator to foreman, Dane felt compelled to micro-manage the activity of the plant.

Dane interviewed three white candidates before Clarence surprisingly asked if he could apply for the job. Dane felt compelled to grant the request of the lean, fit, thirty-something man with the infectious smile who always got his line to meet the deadlines set by Sullivan, no matter how big the order.

To Dane's surprise, Sullivan suggested that he give Clarence, a man with three semesters of post-secondary education, a shot at being foreman. Sullivan argued that it would be good for employee morale and might improve

Anderson, Inc.'s bottom line. Sullivan, sensing Dane's reluctance, put it in terms he'd appreciate. Dane could pay Clarence less than a white man and his new protégé would be none the wiser and forever grateful.

So Clarence got his big break, but contrary to Frank's assertion and Dane's astonishment, a number of his Negroes expressed indignation at the thought of reporting to one of their own. Frederick and Cedric, two young oil vat installers with kinky Afros, protested to anyone who would listen that Clarence wasn't up for the job. Melvin, the shipping dock supervisor, who had the wrinkled face of a Shar-Pei, reminded everyone that he had been at Anderson longer than anyone and was righteously pissed that he hadn't been interviewed. And he wasn't the only voice of dissent. Elmer, the six foot five beanpole forklift driver who had the task of picking up loaded pallets of product from the lines and stacking them on towering warehouse shelves, considered Melvin a mentor. Elmer was afflicted with a bit of a stutter and eyes that crossed. Upon hearing the news of Clarence's promotion he didn't hesitate to spit it out that Dane's choice was a "mis... mis...mis...mis-take...a,a,a, bi-bi-big one." To show his contempt for the decision, Elmer blatantly ignored Clarence's warnings to stop racing through the factory.

The only allies that the new foreman had were line-operator Faye, a plump matronly woman who attended the same church as the Wilson family and Reggie, a long time friend and senior advocate who had the graying temples and withered face to prove it. Reggie's loyalty earned him the line operator position vacated by Clarence's promotion. Line operators made an extra quarter an hour, so the position was highly coveted.

Only Melvyn's job paid more and most considered the nickel differential hardly worth the hassle that came with warehousing and shipping. Melvyn would now have to report to Clarence and that didn't sit well with a man already steamed for being overlooked.

It was a small plant. The salaries of everyone that worked the floor were common knowledge except for that of the foreman, which had always remained a mystery.

As jealousy reared its ugly head, Clarence's dictates were often dismissed with curt epithets. Overall production was off. The situation became so dire that Dane, for the first time ever, questioned Sullivan's sage suggestion and considered replacing Wilson with one of the white candidates he interviewed that had yet to land a job.

Things continued to go bad as Elmer, ignoring Clarence's admonition to slow down, hit a wall with his forklift. From his perch on high, Dane's wrath manifested itself as a primal scream that permeated the entire plant.

"FIRE HIM! FIRE THAT IDIOT NOW!"

Elmer's termination was offset only by the new foreman's quick repair of the damage and a promise made by Elmer, marched into Dane's office by Clarence, that, "it...it...wi..will...nev...nev...never..hap...hap...pen..a...ah...ah... gin...Sor...sor... sor...ry sir." Dane took pity on the errant driver who he had no idea was afflicted with an impediment of speech and crisscrossed eyes. The reprieve won Clarence newfound respect, loyalty and conversion of the unbelievers, including Dane. Production gradually returned to Sullivan levels and the decision to make Clarence foreman proved to be wise counsel after all.

As the months passed, the new foreman continued to surprise Dane. Clarence presented a plan he was sure would enrich the bottom line by improving employee morale.

When Dane laughed at the notion, Clarence presented evidence from a recent work-time-study he discovered at the library. The research confirmed that "employee productivity is intrinsically linked to employee morale." Dane was impressed that his new protégé had embraced the foreman position with zeal. Here was a man passionate about making a difference.

Dane agreed to Clarence's plan, provided it did not cost Anderson Inc. a dime and ultimately improved profitability. Clarence unveiled each new detail of his vision on a series of successive Mondays hoping to instill excitement on a day dreaded by workingmen and women.

Clarence encouraged employees to participate in a weekly potluck lunch of homemade dishes and recipes. Attendance was minimal at first but, in time, participation improved and conviviality between employees of different departments flourished. Even the bachelors had recipes for potato chip dips that they considered worthy of sharing. While staff shared their dishes amongst each other, Clarence listened to employee proposals on how to improve production and create a better workplace. Frank Sullivan never welcomed that kind of input. Not all of the tips were executed, but Anderson employees felt invested.

Based on tips tendered, Clarence changed the start and end times for various shifts and positions. Initially some were reluctant to accept the changes, but as the tinkering came from their peers rather than a boss, employees were more willing to give it a go. As it became apparent that the modifications improved productivity, opposition melted. A result of potluck exchange had the shipping department start their day later than the rest of the plant.

Prior to such changes, shipping had an extended and non-productive morning with an afternoon filled with undue stress as they rushed to get everything packed onto transport. The later morning start provided freight carriers with a traffic flow pattern that was less congested. The atmosphere in shipping improved and so did the service of removing pallets of filled fluid containers stacked at the end of a line, which when not addressed, became an impediment to the line's productivity.

Two of the four vat operators came in a half hour earlier while the other two came in a half hour later from the general start time of 8:00 a.m. In this way, the six lines were ready to go at the moment employees walked in rather than making employees wait for their fill-up tanks to be serviced. The vat operators who came in later, stayed later, ensuring the cleanup of all the vats, thus making the fill-up in the morning smoother. The shift changes made Clarence the first on site and sometimes the last to leave and everyone noticed, including Dane.

Clarence convinced Dane that the two summer jobs should be made available to children related to employees providing the applicants were at least 16 years old, able to get a work permit and willing to do the work. The winning teen-agers would be drawn from a raffle open to employees with sons and daughters, nephews and nieces who met the required conditions. This was a major hit with Anderson employees whether they had kids or not because it shined hope and opportunity. The drawing was set to take place in late May on the six month anniversary of Clarence as foreman, with work to begin in early June for the lucky winners.

Clarence read anything and everything about work flow and found from that study that music could actually energize workers for peak performance. Dane was skeptical but allowed Clarence, with Reggie's help, to wire a turntable into the factory PA system. From his desk, which sat on a raised platform in the front of the factory, Clarence played DJ, spinning jazz, blues and R&B tunes created by artists whose work came to be known as the Chicago Blues Sound. The music vibe helped make the day go faster and productivity continued to increase allowing Dane the assurance that more sales orders could be fulfilled even if that required some overtime, giving employees a chance to make more money, thus paying off for everybody including Anderson, Inc.

Previously the workers only had an unpaid half-hour lunch break but that schedule changed to include two paid fifteen-minute coffee breaks. This was a refreshing change since the tedious rote quality of the work demanded breaks for man and machine, thus insuring personnel safety and extending the life of the motors on each line. The employees appreciated the additional breaks and the fact that they were paid now 8.5 hours per day rather than just 8 or 42.5 hours per week with the 2.5 hours at an overtime rate. For the workers at Anderson, the additional sorely needed dollars and the promise of overtime compensation energized the ranks. Without expressing it, Dane was pleasantly surprised by the increased output of his factory, since he had always considered his Negroes a bit lazy.

As sales orders increased, Clarence requested from Dane an additional four hours of production to meet the new demands.   A survey regarding when the additional hours should be scheduled was taken at a potluck lunch.   The overtime was designated for Tuesdays and Thursdays with days starting at 8:00 a.m. and finishing at 7:00 p.m.   Things were going Clarence's way or so he thought until his world and that of John Beriso's collided.

"But suppose God is black? What if we go to Heaven and we, all our lives, have treated the Negro as an inferior, and God is there, and we look up and He is not white? What then is our response?"

\- Robert Francis Kennedy

CHAPTER TWO

LOST IN THE KITCHEN

A bell by a red phone on the watch table jingled, activating an alarm klaxon that called the men of Truck 13 to action.

From portraits hung high on a wall, the eyes of the president, the governor and the mayor, appeared to gaze upon first responders scurrying to put on their gear as they jumped onto Truck 13, a hook and ladder and Engine 26, a shiny red pumper.

In the kitchen, Chief John Beriso, a tall beefy built man of 45, untied his white apron and flung it on a chair next to a table full of half-finished ravioli. The Chief utilized his culinary talent to entertain family, friends and woo the men of Truck 13.

The Irish-American brigade initially bucked the thought of having an Italian as their boss until they tasted his food.

Beriso was one of a handful of firemen, without an Irish surname who had captured the brass ring of Battalion Chief. He had done so at the relatively young age of 35. Beriso's battalion of ten firehouses with a contingency of 150 men had the hefty responsibility of protecting Chicago's oldest factories tied to families of distinction. There were rumors that Blackie, a moniker for Beriso, not only had the backing of powerful Alderman Danny Kells, Chicago's Deputy-Mayor, but also the patronage of his godfather, Alfonso Romano, an operative who enjoyed cache with the powerful, be they saints or sinners from the Cardinal's office to the politicians and mobsters who made it happen in the town that "Billy Sunday could not shut down."

At Truck 13, the Chief's house, there was an implicit mandate that everyone had to take a turn cooking. With Blackie in-house and the challenge of pleasing the finicky taste buds of fire fighters, those who didn't know how to prepare a meal were more than willing to take tips from a chief who cooked like a chef. Beriso had learned the art of cooking at the hands of his mother, Rose, who upon her arrival in America found employment in the kitchen of one of Chicago's finest Italian restaurants, Gene & Georgetti's at the corner of Wells Street and Illinois, under Chicago's beloved if not noisy L, short for elevated train.

As an officer, Beriso need never cook again but he enjoyed making dinner at least once a month for his own house and that of another house in the district. Breaking bread was a way to garner esteem, foster morale and solicit ideas on how to deal with harms way that his men faced day in and day out. Within his first year as a Battalion Chief, Beriso had shared his culinary skills with every house in his battalion. The suppers paid off. His heritage became a non-issue with men who developed a bond with a no-nonsense commander they respected yet feared, willing to die in battle, rather than curry his disfavor. The Chief repeated a phrase that became a mantra for his fighting Irish. "From the Greeks comes the word professional; a humanitarian that helps others. Be proud! That's what we do, that's who we are."

And if you didn't like the Chief that was okay, providing you never questioned his judgment while fighting the beast and subsequently the back draft that harkens in the belly of every inferno. The men trusted their Chief to ensure their safety above the demands of brass. Beriso's record as an officer, be it as an Engineer, a Lieutenant, and a Captain and now as a Chief was impeccable; not a man, in his charge, had ever been lost when he was on the scene. As a manager, Beriso treated men that made an honest mistake with constructive criticism that at times stung. The explosive temper only reared its head for those that violated policy. Even then punishment was fair and swift.

No one wanted to be in Blackie's dog house; a nickname given the Chief as a young officer for his devotion to a Dalmatian who was more black than white.

Blackie, the dog, was legendary for having saved a baby at a fire that ultimately cost the canine his life. From that day forth, Beriso never allowed a dog in any house that he controlled as a lieutenant or captain.

Only Truck 17 and Engine Company 26 had Dalmatians that were there on the day Beriso became Chief of the 5th. Out of respect for the memory of Blackie, no lieutenant or captain in the 5th had the heart to ask the Chief for permission to replace a dog. And so with time and attrition, Battalion 5 became dog less.

As the klaxon blared and the trucks roared, Beriso slid into the shotgun seat of his official car marked, "Chief of the 5th Battalion." Charlie McGann, a carrot-topped 50-year-old Irish-Catholic with a touch of brogue served officially as the Chief's "wheel man" and unofficially as his trusted confidant. McGann flipped on the bubble, activated the siren and lead the charge of a battery of fire apparatus onto the street racing to a blaze.

The radio squawked.

"Base to Battalion Five."

Beriso grabbed the radio microphone.

"Five to Base."

Squawk.

"Chief, you will have an escort. National Guard troops."

Beriso looked puzzled. He turned to Charlie who shrugged as he pressed the button to respond.

"What's up? I've been in the kitchen."

Squawk.

"Martin Luther Coon, King, was shot. You guys didn't have the TV or the radio on in the kitchen?"

The Chief shook his head before depressing the switch. He didn't want to admit once again that he was out of touch with the world when he cooked.

"10-4 base. Thanks for the escort."

Squawk.

"Don't thank me. Thank Mayor Daley. He's ordered a 'shoot to kill for looters.' Just be careful out there."

Charlie and the Chief's eyes rolled, followed by a look that only close partners of ten years share. Charlie spoke first.

"It must be awfully good."

"Red, I don't have the foggiest notion-

"Chief you do know the fuck what I'm talking about. You get lost when you cook. You know you're going to have to kill me now. But make it look like an accident at the fire. My kids will get more."

Beriso didn't want to hear Charlie's bitching.

"Charlie, you can bet your ass I'll make it look good."

Charlie whipped the car onto a sidewalk and back onto the street to avoid a car double-parked. The trucks following had to pull into the oncoming lanes forcing vehicles to the side but the impediment slowed their movement as the Chief's car pulled ahead.

"Despite the invincibility myth that you perpetuate for the rookies, I know the one chink in your armor, Blackie."

The men exchanged glances as Charlie avoided pedestrians who strayed too far into the street. Charlie continued.

"You know, 'the my shit doesn't stink myth,' because unlike you boobs I know what the fuck I'm doing even when you don't."

Beriso was about to start when Charlie stopped him.

"Not a fucking word Chief, please. Your secret is safe with me."

Beriso resigned any effort to protest.

"Well thank sweet Jesus I've got you as a confidant."

A good driver was worth his weight in gold because he was so much more. Charlie McGann, was also a bookkeeper, a secretary, and an able diplomat who knew how to negotiate on behalf of the entire battalion for whatever it needed from paper clips to state-of-the-art equipment. He was the perfect attaché for a man like Beriso.

With McGann by his side, Beriso didn't feel alone. He knew that at least someone in his command had the experience and the balls to call it like he saw it and if necessary remind the Chief that he was human - just like his men.

———

"I said to him very emphatically and very definitely that an order be issued by him immediately to shoot to kill any arsonist or anyone with a Molotov cocktail in his hand, because they're potential murderers, and to shoot to maim or cripple anyone looting."

Richard J. Daley – April 1968
-- Publicly recounting to the press his instructions to Chicago's Chief of Police.

"There wasn't any shoot to kill order. That was a fabrication."

Richard J. Daley – Later that same month (reaction to media coverage of the "shoot to kill," quote.)

"They have vilified me, they have crucified me; yes, they have even criticized me."

Richard J. Daley - Additional reaction to media coverage.

CHAPTER THREE

A TALE OF TWO CITIES

The kit included a twenty-two inch bass, a snare, two side tom-toms, a floor tom-tom and Zildjian high-hat, crash and ride cymbals. Joe popped up from behind the bass drum as he finished attaching a Slingerland pedal to its rim.

The pedal's performance did not please the young man. He vowed to himself that as soon as he had the money he'd replace it with an expensive Rogers, used exclusively by his idol, celebrated drummer Buddy Rich. Joe was one of only fourteen teens who qualified to attend a clinic given by Mr. Rich at Frank & Sal's Drum Shop in downtown Chicago. It was a select group of young men, all currently taking instruction with a working noted musician, proficient at reading drum charts and flashy in their solo performances which had been judged by the owners, Frank and Sal Buoniconti. The event drew a good deal of media attention due to Buddy's celebrity and the fact that the owners were savvy enough to stage it on a Saturday, typically a slow news day in Chicago. Joe wanted to be just like Buddy but, for the moment, he had to be content playing rock with a group of local teens.

The front head of Joe's bass drum was embossed with a floral psychedelic pattern of letters that read, "The Vague Traces." The Traces were lead by Satch Olecky, a pock-marked rhythm guitarist with too-tall shy Mike Cass on bass, wise-ass pretty boy Brian Ratke on lead guitar and Joe behind the drums. The four young men had assembled in the Beriso basement to practice for their upcoming gig, a birthday party scheduled for the next evening.

Finding a place to practice was always difficult since the band, with its array of VOX amplifiers, the same amps the Beatles used, was any parent's nightmare. The band members took turns hosting the practices. At Joe's house they could only practice when Mr. Beriso was absent for the day working his 24-hour firehouse shift. Joe's old man hated rock music, considered it nothing but noise and a waste of time.

Mrs. Beriso's take was a bit different. She saw the band as an activity that kept the kids off the streets and out of gang trouble. She permitted her son and his band mates to practice whenever John was working, providing they followed a few simple rules.

Instruments were to be turned off at 8 p.m. sharp on a weekday, 9 p.m. for a weekend. The boys had to pick up after themselves, not leaving a mess in the basement. They were expected to leave the neighborhood quietly and absolutely could not smoke in the basement or anywhere on the Beriso property.

Moving the equipment was a pain, so with Mr. Beriso gone two to three times a week, it was just easier to practice when he worked. So unofficially the Beriso basement became band headquarters for "The Vague Traces." John Beriso knew of the arrangement and also had a condition that he insisted be met. Satch, Brian and Mike's parents had to write a note stating that the Beriso household, should it be robbed, was not responsible for replacing the expensive guitars and/or amps. Gloria knew of the condition and initially suggested that her husband include the caveat that if a fire occurred, the family would not be liable. John absolutely bristled at the notion that a fire could break out in his house and nixed the suggestion.

Once a month, girls were allowed to visit and watch the band for their last hour of practice providing they respect the same rules governing the boys. When girls did appear, Mrs. Beriso's presence was always nearby, washing and drying the family's clothes in machines that sat on the opposite side of the basement. The boys expressed their exasperation at her need to chaperone by singing the hook to The Buckinghams' hit, "Kind Of A Drag." But the presence of girls also had rewards. "Mrs. B," as she was affectionately called by the kids, prepared an extra-large delicious homemade pizza with sausage and pepperoni, served with ice cold Cokes on nights with a female audience. It was idyllic until that evening of April 4, 1968.

On that day, practice began as usual a few minutes before six p.m. with the *Stone's*, "Satisfaction." It was a tune that allowed Brian to check the fuzz box, Satch a chance to check the microphone mix and Mike and Joe an opportunity to fine-tune the bass line. The Traces had the number down and enjoyed playing it as their opener at party gigs or sock-hops because it immediately got the venue rocking.

"The Vague Traces" were into the chorus when the light at the bottom of the stairs flipped on and off, a signal to immediately cease playing. As the music died, Joe and his mates looked to the stairs. Usually Mrs. B would yell down that she had a phone call or that there was a visitor at the door. But this time there was nothing but the background buzz of a television. While the denizens of the basement were wondering, the voice of Mrs. B. cut through the silence, "Boys, come up now!"

As Joe climbed off his stool, Satch, Brian and Mike ditched their guitars. Something serious was up. They rushed up the stairs to find Mrs. B in the front room sitting on a large sofa with her eyes glued to the set, the centerpiece of a fine furniture cabinet that featured a hi-fi stereo and a 32-inch color television. Walter Chronkite, the eminent but avuncular CBS anchor regarded by the public as the most trusted man in America, delivered somberly in black and white, the news of the hour. Color TV transmission in Chicago at that time was available on NBC and WGN but more Americans, color not withstanding, turned to Walter for their news.

Satch and Brian slid next to Mrs. B on the sofa. Mike took the Lazy-Boy chair that was normally reserved for Mr. Beriso as Joe grabbed a spot on the carpet, plopping up against his mom's legs. Mrs. B fidgeted to move her legs to the outside of her son's back.

Joe wondered aloud, "What Ma?"

"Shh," said Mrs. B. "They shot Martin Luther King."

Chronkite continued over the drone of Teletype machines ticking away. "Dr. King was standing on the balcony of a second floor hotel room tonight when according to a companion, and I quote, 'Shots was fired from across the street. The bullet exploded in his face.'" Walter adjusted his glasses. He had done the same exact move when he reported the sad news of JFK's assassination. It gave Mr. Chronkite a moment to regain composure, be resolute and hold back tears that welled in his eyes. He then continued. "Memphis police, had been keeping a close watch over the Nobel peace prize winner because of a turbulent racial situation, arrived on the scene immediately. They rushed the 39-year-old Negro leader to a hospital where he died of a bullet wound in the neck. Police said they found a high-powered hunting rifle about a block from the hotel. It was not immediately identified as the murder weapon. Mayor Henry Loeb has reinstated the dusk to dawn curfew he imposed on the city last week when a March lead by King erupted in violence. Governor Buford Ellington has called out four thousand National Guardsmen. King's murder has touched off sporadic acts of violence in the Negro part of the city. There are reports of trouble also in other cities."

The phone sitting on a small end table next to Mrs. B rang, interrupting the CBS News. Joe immediately moved to turn the TV down as his mother picked up the phone. "Hello. Beriso residence."

Mrs. B nodded as she listened. "I know Roberta, we're watching the news now. You don't say. Carl has to report to the armory? Oh, my God, this is what we've feared." Mrs. B put her hand over the mouthpiece as she shared the news with the boys. "Roberta's husband must report to duty. Riots."

Mrs. B gave the call her full attention. "Oh my God, no." she took a deep breath, "that's John's district."

She drew a deep breath as she continued to listen.

"Of course, I'll keep the boys in. Although I'm sure we're safe on the northwest side. Damn that King! He's just as Mayor Daley pegged him, 'An agitator who will ruin the quilt that makes up our city and our nation...the quilt is separate and apart, that's what allows us to live in peace even with our differences.'"

Mrs. B listened for a moment and then burst into laughter.

"Agreed Roberta...our precinct captain is here all the time, so I better have at least one Daley quote to impress him ...right?"

In Chicago, every neighborhood had a precinct captain who made sure that the faithful voted the way the Daley machine wanted them to vote. In return, your precinct captain could grant you a favor, a city service or even in some cases a job. The precinct captain answered to the committeeman, the ward boss, who in most cases was much more powerful than the alderman seated in the city council.

Mrs. B listened intently, nodded and uttered, "Ah-hah, Carl told you that? They haven't said a word about that on the news, at least not yet. Oh my God, that's terrible. My prayers are with Carl and you. Don't hesitate to call me, if you need to talk."

As soon as Mrs. B hung up the phone, the boys turned to her for more. "According to Sergeant Petersen, Whites have been pulled from their cars and beaten by Negroes upset with King being shot. They're rioting on the west side including your father's district. I hope your father's okay. Mrs. B's eyes watered with tears. Resolute, she whispered softly but audibly, "And Vince, needs to let us know he's safe in Urbana?"

"I doubt if they're rioting at the U of I, Mom. It's a college town. Are there even any slums there?"

"I don't know, Joe. Let's hope you're right. Dammit, I wish the men of this family would take a minute to call."

Mrs. B wiped the corner of her eye to prevent a tear from raining on her cheek. She took a deep breath and focused on the boys in her living room. "As to the rest of you, none of you should leave. It's not safe. Call your parents and I'll talk with them and together we'll figure out the best way to get you home."

Across town on Chicago's south side, a svelte attractive Jackie Wilson snuggled her children, nine-year-old pig-tailed Hailey and eight year old Clarence Jr., a spitting image of his dad, as they sat on the living room couch. Together, they watched with awe as Walter Chronkite delivered the news that Martin Luther King had been assassinated. As film appeared on the screen, Walter's voice could be heard, "Just in, film from one of our cameramen capturing the wanton destruction of Harlem, New York." The sound on the TV was audible but diminished as they focused on the sound from the radio on top of the 32 inch television with its antenna set high in the air, tuned to radio station, WVON (the Voice Of the Negro).

"Contrary to reports made by white media commentators and politicians, Dr. King was not, I repeat WAS NOT, an agitator revving up Negroes for no good but rather in Memphis to lend support to a sanitation workers strike. Dr. King was there because the Memphis City Council and Mayor Loeb, refused to be fair and honest in its dealings with its public servants, the sanitation workers, that coincidentally are predominately Negro."

The sound from V-O-N - the voice of the Negro continued. "Even President Johnson and AFL-CIO President George Meany offered their assistance in resolving the dispute only to have Mayor Loeb turn them down. But is anyone calling LBJ or Mr. Meany agitators?"

"Ironically Reverend King delivered last night, at Mason Temple, before a packed house of striking sanitation workers a speech which I predict will be forever remembered. Let me play a portion of the recording of that speech by Dr. King."

A click of a switch preceded the distinctive voice of Martin Luther King. "Like anybody, I would like to live a long life. Longevity has its place. But I'm not concerned about that now. I just want to do God's will. And He's allowed me to go up the mountain. And I've looked over.

And I've seen the Promised Land. I may not get there with you. But I want you to know tonight, that we, as a people, will get to the Promised Land. And I'm happy, tonight. I'm not worried about anything. I'm not fearing any man. Mine eyes have seen the glory of the coming of the Lord."

For a split second there was silence on the radio. Then the opening notes of "Mine Eyes Have Seen the Coming of the Lord," or known officially as "The Battle Hymn of the Republic" filled the airwaves. The music was in stark contrast with the images on the TV of fires, windows being smashed and National Guardsman with bayonets drawn marching towards a mob of angry black people.

Clarence's mother, Deidre, a heavy set woman in her mid-sixties pushed through a swing door that separated the kitchen from the dining area. Her hands were full as she carried serving dishes filled with the food she had prepared for dinner. "Y'all know we don't have that TV on once supper's ready. Y'all get over here before this food gets cold!"

Deidre's face turned stern as she watched her daughter-in-law and grandchildren ignore her. This was not going to do. She instinctively knew something was amiss. She slowly moved towards the front room to see why the lack of respect. The film of rioting dissolved to a portrait of Martin Luther King with the dates 1929-1968 displayed in the lower third of the screen as the music from the radio played on.

"Oh, my God," she whispered and yet her words registered with each soul in the room. "They done killed him?" Her eyes welled and then the tears poured down her rough hewn black skin weathered by a life of work, intolerance and sacrifice.

Jackie peered into Deidre's eyes. Deidre could read the irises of Jackie's eyes. The answer without so much as a nod of the head was an immortal yes.

Deidre openly sobbed choking out the words, "Oh my Lord. This is just like when I was a little girl in Tulsa."

Hailey took her grandma's hand in hers and asked, "What happened in Tulsa, Grandma?"

"The city came down. Good black men, like our lovable Doc, were mass murdered just because they were colored."

Junior ran to Jackie's lap for protection. "Is that gonna happen to us, Mama?"

"Let's pray not, honey." Realizing she had done little to assure her son, she followed with, "Absolutely not."

Deidre stepped over to the TV and radio. She turned off the radio. "I don't need to know what WVON is saying. But I do needs to know what the great white uncle, Mister Cronkite is saying about us."

Deidre raised the sound of Walter Cronkite's voice over the infamous photo on the screen of Dr. King lying in a pool of blood on the balcony of the Lorraine Motel after being shot. "This AP photo came courtesy of our Memphis affiliate. It appears to be Dr. Martin Luther King seconds after being hit - his aides pointing in the direction of where the fatal bullet may have come from."

There was silence as the picture of Dr. King dying on that balcony began to fade slowly, ever so slowly to black.

———

"I remember the last time we were together, at my home,
shortly before he was murdered. He seemed quite agitated
and preoccupied, and I asked him what the problem was:
'I've come upon something that disturbs me deeply,' he said.
' We have fought hard and long for integration, as I believe
we should have, and I know that we will win.   But I've
come to believe we're integrating into a burning house.'"

\-   Harry Belafonte
(Recalling a conversation with M.L.K.)

CHAPTER FOUR

LET IT BURN

The red strobe lights showered reflections off the wet jet-black pavement on which two fire trucks sat at an angle to each other. Flames spewed from a building painting a silhouette of apparatus appearing to be unmanned. Hoses attached to the pumper, known as "lines" in the trade, lay limp on the street.

A puddle mirrored the arrival of a red chief's car labeled 5th Battalion. Out of the car stepped big John Beriso. He looked quizzically at the limp hoses and snapped, "Why the hell aren't these lines pumping water? Where the fuck is everybody?"

A fireman crawled out from under one of the trucks, grabbed the Chief and pulled him to the ground as gun shots rang out. "Chief, get down!"

Under the truck John discovered all the other fireman seeking shelter from a rain of death by fire, not the kind of fire they were prepared to combat. That other kind of fire had always been reserved for "THE MAN" but never for the FIREMAN, who was always till today, EVERY MAN's best friend.

Charlie McGann momentarily froze as a bullet shattered the rooftop bubble light on the car. McGann spun out pulling away as fast as his Chevy engine cranked torque to whisk him out of range.

Upon McGann's exit, National Guard troops pulled up in two jeeps, jumped out and returned fire. One of the bullets met its mark spraying a black face red. The others on the roof worked as a team to cover two black men who immediately jumped to drag their wounded comrade away from the line of fire. The insurgents retreated.

A National Guardsman dashed under the trucks. "Who's in charge?"

To his left, the guardsman heard, "I am."

The guardsman turned and acknowledged Beriso. "We're trying to clear them out, sir! But if we can't, just let it burn. Damn niggers!"

The Chief reiterated the command, "That's it. Let it burn! We've got another call. Guardsman, we could use an escort. What do you say Sarge?"

The guardsman laughed. "I'm a corporal but I'm the only one above private so..." the corporal saluted noting John's rank, "you've got it Chief."

The Chief jumped into the cab of one of the trucks.

A fire fighter would have to ride standing up in the back. The Guard plastered the roofline with a volley of lead as the trucks pulled out.

The Chief picked up the radio and called McGann.

"Charlie, you okay? We're headed to 2200 West Polk Street."

The squawk box crackled with McGann's voice.

"That's one of ours, right Chief?"

"Yeah, Red. They've lit the factory zone of the 5th."

Industry on west Polk Street where Anderson Inc. resided was under siege as rioters moved into the district lobbing one Molotov cocktail after another at the buildings.

Anderson, Inc. was in jeopardy as the rioters targeted the northern plantations of rich white owned factories.

* * *

As the beer bottle smashed a window at the top of the bi-fold doors of Anderson Inc., an incendiary mixture of gasoline and spark erupted into an explosive fireball that ignited both the interior and exterior sides of the entrance. A collective gasp erupted from the workers of Anderson, not knowing whether to run or fight. If the fire spread to the chemical vats hanging above the six production lines, Anderson would explode and become a raging inferno fueled by petrochemicals.

Clarence yelled over the PA mic, "Shut it down, now!"

The various operators immediately hit emergency cut off switches that brought the factory to a standstill. Dane, oblivious to the angry crowds out on the street, raised his window from his perch on high. "Why are we shutting down on an overtime Thursday? What's going on Clarence?"

Clarence, Reggie and Elmer ignored the questions as they grabbed extinguishers from cases strapped to pillars. Reggie and Elmer sprayed the inside of the doors as Clarence stepped outside to combat the fire of an unruly mob cheering as the front of Anderson burned.

The rioters, some with torches in their hands illuminated the dark blue skies turning black with night. Clarence was the butt of catcalls and ethnic excrement. "Working for the man...ya porch nigger?"

Another called out, "Yeah, you the Uncle-Tom of this place."

The epithets continued to rain, "The Master must love you, did he fuck your mama?"

Clarence snuffed out the flames licking the front door, unmoved by the rhetoric of the mob when he noticed a rioter about to light the wick of another Molotov cocktail. "Want to eat that?" Clarence asked.

The rioter scowled back. "What you talkin' porch monkey?"

Clarence pointed the extinguisher nozzle at the angry man's face. "You're barking up the wrong tree!"

Clarence continued to hold the man at bay, suddenly fearful that he might have to spray him. Without moving the nozzle, Clarence rotated his head to face the rest of the crowd. "This place is run and operated by colored, just like you, who need to keep their jobs."

"That's bullshit," yelled a tall black with a huge Afro and a face filled with scars from a life in the ghetto.

"We know Anderson ain't no black man even if you're his nigger. He should pay for King's blood."

Clarence looked amazed and a bit stunned.

Afro shouted for all to hear, "You in the dark, darkie? They done killed King." He looked back at the mob. "He don't know. The fool don't know what's happened. Are they all in the dark?"

The bi-fold doors opened as Elmer and Reggie held their nozzles high, poised to counter any flicker that Clarence may have missed. Anderson's workers stepped forward staring back at the crowd as they witnessed the destruction of their block. The two factories to the north were burning. The storefront windows of the abandoned buildings across the street were shattered. Garbage was everywhere and any car that was not parked in a lot with a protective fence had been trashed. Dane allowed Clarence's music but he forbid radio or TV, anywhere in the plant, including his office.

"Why?" asked Faye peering at the man with the Afro. "We need to keep our jobs to feed our families."

"Don't you people listen to the radio? Dr. King was shot down like a dog in Memphis by whitey, less than an hour ago. He's dead."

Faye and her colleagues put their hands to their heads, covered their mouths with astonishment and wept. The crowd became still, moved by the loss, grief, pain, sadness and hurt of people stunned and unaware of the news. They saw themselves - before the bile and mercurial taste of hatred choked them with rage. The man holding the Molotov put his lighter away. Clarence dropped his extinguisher. It rattled and rolled on the concrete apron twisting and turning.

Sirens echoed and red light effervescently flashed from the darkness of the viaduct, the infamous demarcation set by *The Watchdogs*. The jeeps rolled out first with a guardsman standing in each of the vehicles, rifles raised to the sky. The fire trucks followed with the 5th Battalion Chief's car in the rear. A pothole jarred one of the jeeps and a shot discharged.

The mob scattered. Anderson's employees ran back into the plant seeking cover. A Molotov cocktail sailed through the open doorway striking a pallet of cartons containing cans ready to be filled with fluids. A fireball erupted and the blaze quickly spread to Clarence's platform. Reggie and Elmer sprayed fire retardant only to find their extinguishers quickly emptied. "Shit! They're dry!" yelled Reggie. The blaze quickly spread.

Clarence couldn't find the extinguisher he dropped. He rushed down the front apron, into the street, waving his arms as he forced the fire trucks to slam on their brakes. "Stop, stop!"

A guardsman jumped from his jeep and clubbed Clarence with a baton. Clarence dropped to the ground, moaning as he held his bleeding head.

Chief John Beriso bolted from the lead truck. "Forget 'em down the street. It's lost. Let's try and save," the Chief looked up and saw, "Anderson's."

Clarence looked up to see the man standing over him barking out commands as his men quickly scurried to hook up a hose line from the engine pumper to a hydrant. The Chief continued to bark. "Move it! Hose any nigger that gets in the way!"

Clarence's eyes locked onto the cold face of an angry, stressed Beriso. The gunfire had taken its toll.

Anderson employees, shocked by the news and the bizarre events unfolding in front of them, were slow to scatter as a jet blast from a water canon doused the pallet of burning cartons. Employees soaked and socked on their ass evoked cackling from some of the firemen. Another blast pummeled Clarence's desk tossing clipboards, papers and the record player to the floor. Within seconds the threat disappeared, as did the flames.

"Shut it down and pack it in!" barked Beriso. "Take it down the street. Contain 'em so the embers don't ignite something on the other side. Charlie will bring me down."

McGann drove the chief's car up onto the sidewalk as he coasted onto the apron of the plant. Dane bolted from his office to the floor inspecting the damage and checking on employees drenching wet. He stopped when Beriso approached. "What the hell's going on Captain?"

"You mean Chief, don't you? Saving this plant! Who the hell are you?"

"Dane Anderson, the owner. Look, I appreciate all you guys do but what do your men find so funny?"

The Chief cut Dane off. "We're done here. But I'll be back Anderson. You've got violations, loads of 'em, and I don't need to answer to you. Not today."

* * *

A month later the acrid smell of smoke continued to infuse the block of Anderson, Inc; it was the only factory still standing and operational on Polk Street.

Business was brisk at Jimmy & Gina's Italian Beef since other eateries, not protected by a viaduct location, were destroyed. Reconstruction had commenced so there were plenty of lunchtime clients with hard hats. Daley was determined to prove that his city would bounce back; that Chicago was indisputably, "The city that works."

Outside the diner, atop a ladder, one of Gina's busboys carefully scraped off "Jimmy &," from the "Jimmy and Gina's Italian Beef" logo painted on the front window. Patrons entering the diner avoided walking under the ladder for fear of bad luck. There had been more than enough of that with the riots. As the busboy finished his task, a fire chief's car pulled up and parked.

John and Charlie exited the car and entered a diner filled exclusively with white customers. The men grabbed two seats at the counter next to Police Captain Patrick O'Malley, a blond blue-eyed die-hard thirty-something bachelor and his Sancho Panza, Lieutenant O'Reilly, a father of seven, married for over twelve years. O'Malley and O'Reilly graduated together from the police academy.

"Chief and Charlie – how's it hanging? You remember Lieutenant O'Reilly."

"Sure," responded Charlie.

It was Patrick's turn. "Guys, we're keeping those hydrants clear at Cabrini for you."

Charlie nodded recognition. The Chief shook O'Reilly's hand.

"Thanks." The Chief followed with, "As you know, it's always tough fighting one in the projects."

A busboy carrying a tray full of water glasses placed two in front of John and Charlie. Two small children ran behind the busboy almost knocking the tray out of his hand. They burst through the swing doors into the kitchen.

"Dino, Mia, stop goofing around. Put that rag on the counter son. And young lady, did you forget? You're supposed to fill the napkin holders."

Gina Castronova, a striking 32 year old widow with green eyes, a great rack, silky auburn tresses and an alluring Italian accent flashed sweet serene smiles at her sunshine, her five-year-old son and four-year-old daughter. The kids returned their momma's smile. Their grandmother, Renata, who helped her daughter with the cooking, gave each of them a squeeze.

"Mommy, the Chief and Charlie just sat down."

"Thanks, I'll be right out. Now go."

The kids exited the kitchen intent on pleasing their mom. With the death of their father, Jimmy, Gina became sole parent and sole proprietor of "Jimmy & Gina's Italian Beef."

Gina followed her kids through the doors. Without a moment of hesitation she filled a glass full of soda and placed it in front of the captain.

"Here you go, Cap."

"Thanks, sugar."

Gina then moved over to John and Charlie and gave each man an over-the-counter buss on their cheeks. She pulled out a pen and put it to an order pad.

"Two of my favorite men. What are you having?"

John glanced at the busboy scraping the window. "Your dropping 'Jimmy' from the name of your place?"

Gina looked up from her pad. "It's over two years. It's time. Beefs, gents?"

Charlie nodded yes. Gina marked her pad.

John turned his focus from the window scraping to Gina. "Make it two for me, with one to go, okay?"

"You got it Chief. Coffee?" Both men nodded yes.

Gina grabbed coffee cups with saucers and placed them in front of the firemen. She turned to pick up a potful of coffee on a four-pot-warming stand and filled their cups with steaming hot java. O'Malley followed the wiggle of her hips as she put the pot back and headed to the kitchen. "A window opens."

Lieutenant O'Reilly tapped O'Malley to look across the room and notice Mia and Dino. "Be careful, she's got baggage, Cap."

"I'll make an exception," smiled O'Malley.

John, Charlie, and O'Reilly laughed.

"Who're you kidding?" asked McGann. "You're a fricking Baskin Robbins with all thirty-nine flavors on your horizon."

"Yeah, but I'm not getting any younger," O'Malley winked. "It's time for me to settle down."

"All in the past, huh, Cap?

"Of course, but enough about me Charlie. I've been hearing big things about your boss down at City Hall."

Charlie patted John on the back. "The big lug's up for Division Marshall."

John sheepishly smiled. "Nothing set in stone."

"Say you don't want it," pressed O'Reilly.

John ignored the pressure. He took a long sip of coffee.

O'Malley raised his soda in a toast. "I'm impressed."

Both John and Charlie smiled at the gesture. O'Malley then turned to John. "But I got to tell you Chief, and please don't take this the wrong way, the first time you took the reins of the 5th Battalion, I wondered whether you could make the grade."

John's right eyelid raised waiting for O'Malley's explanation.

"You know, being a dago; asked to command Irishmen?"

Charlie's smile vanished as Gina served the firemen their orders on white diner plates. "Here you go boys."

"Gina, on second thought can you make our orders to go?" asked John. "Also, that second beef needs sweet peppers."

O'Malley laughed, "One no longer does the job, huh Chief?"

Gina picked up the plates, "No problem Chief," and returned to the kitchen.

O'Malley tried to pat John's stomach only to have the Chief swat the Captain's hand. O'Malley winced. "Feisty? If you're not careful you're going to spill out of those trousers."

John glared at O'Malley.

Charlie sensing the tension chimed in, "C'mon guys."

"For your information O'Malley, one of those beefs isn't for me."

O'Malley smiled. "Who you greasing Chief?"

"In Chicago you never ask who," chastised Charlie.

John rose, ignoring O'Malley. "I got to take a piss Charlie." Charlie waited till his boss entered the bathroom.

"What's wrong with you O'Malley?"

O'Malley sheepishly smiled. "The dago thing kinda slipped."

Charlie shook his head in disgust. "That dago saved your old man when he got caught in an explosion. It was Beriso who dragged his ass out, and let me tell you, your father, a captain, I respected, was unmerciful when it came to that dago. He did everything to break Beriso when he was a rookie."

O'Malley's eyes shined with amazement. "My old man? You're kidding? He never mentioned that."

Charlie shook his head in disbelief. "Obviously you don't know the half of it, but I was there. Your father, Beriso and I went into a smoldering warehouse that stored pistachio nuts. I never knew that pistachios are highly prone to spontaneous combustion. That's why I can't eat 'em. Anyway, we found a night watchman overcome by smoke. I carried him out. Your dad and Beriso continued to look for other civilians and that's when the place exploded. I don't know how that dago, bleeding badly with cuts and bruises all over him, found the strength to pull rubble off your old man and then carry him out, but he did. Your old man owes his life to that WOP, so if you're smart you'll never call him that again, at least not to his face."

The kitchen doors swung open to reveal Gina holding a white bag in her hands. She spotted the Chief walk out of the bathroom returning to the counter. She held up the bag to indicate his order was ready.

Beriso stopped behind Charlie. "Let's go partner."

The Chief pulled a sawbuck from his wallet and handed it to Gina. She rang up the order and slipped John some change.

John turned back to the counter to acknowledge O'Reilly, "Lieutenant." Ignoring Captain O'Malley's look of good-bye, the Chief headed for the door. Charlie shot O'Malley a look of disappointment as he followed his boss.

Disturbed by the cold shoulder, O'Malley wondered aloud, "What?"

A slammed door answered the question unequivocally.

On the other side of the door John and Charlie headed for the Chief's car parked underneath the viaduct. "Fuckin' mick! No offense Charlie."

"None taken Chief. The man doesn't understand that merit demands respect."

"Fuckin' A!" The Chief smiled a look of appreciation at his partner. "For a fuckin' mick, you're okay."

Both men burst into laughter. A flash of lightning lit up the dark viaduct.

"Charlie, I'm going to walk the block to Anderson's."

Thunder exploded and rumbled through the underpass.

"You sure Chief. It looks like rain."

"Yeah. I need to cool off before I see Anderson. I trust you'll be in front enjoying your lunch."

"Take your time Chief. Jimmy and Gina's beefs," Red paused as he and John took in the change of the signage. "Correction, Gina's beefs are better eaten slowly."

———

CHAPTER FIVE

LAY-AWAY TO AP EXAM

The screech of Chicago's elevated trains and the thunder of the skies shook the windows of Frank's Drum Shop. Inside the store, a few shoppers noticed the rattle but not Joe Beriso. Joe was in a zone as he performed some tasty licks on a drum kit, alternating a stick pattern between the tom-toms and a foot pedal pounding a twenty-four inch bass drum. The proprietor, Frank Buoniconti, left his perch behind the counter to get a closer look at Joe's intensity as he finished. "That's some mean action between the toms and that bass."

"It's the pedal, Frank. I can't do this on my set with my Slingerland pedal."

"Well, that's the new one from Gretsch, son. It's got great action and frankly I think it's as good as a Rodgers, maybe better. If you'd like Joe, I can put one aside for you on lay-a-way."

"I can't afford that. That pedal's fifty bucks."

"Maybe your old man can buy it for you, for your graduation."

"How? My old man knows nothing about drums."

"Your brother's coming home from college any day now, right? Get him to tell your dad."

"I already gave Vince a hint, but I told you how he feels about me playing the drums."

Frank persisted. "I've only got three left."

Joe twirled a stick in his right hand and then placed both sticks down on the floor tom-tom. He looked again at the pedal. Frank removed from a glass display a brand new shiny Gretsch drum pedal. He knew how to reel in a sale. "This one could be yours."

Joe longingly looked at the pedal. "I only got five dollars."

"That'll work. After you start your summer job, you can pay down the rest."

"Providing I find a job. Caputo's, the grocery my brother and I worked at last summer burned during the riots."

Frank grabbed a tag and wrote with a black marker in large lettering the name Joe Beriso. He held it up to tempt Joe. "So do I hold it or not?"

Joe reached into his wallet and pulled out a fin leaving a solo dollar, just enough for carfare home. He reluctantly handed the currency to Frank.

"Congratulations Joe, you won't regret it."

Frank fastened the tag, "Joe Beriso - lay-a-way, $45 due," to the precious pedal and placed it on a rack.

Joe focused on the $45 due. He winced.

"C'mon, if you don't get the job, you're only out a fin."

"More than that Frank. I need a job for college expenses otherwise I'm not starting university this fall."

Joe looked up at the clock on the wall. "Is that right?"

Frank checked the time. "It's five minutes fast."

"Wow, I lost track of the time. I've got to get to DePaul within the next fifteen minutes."

"Their downtown campus is only a half-a-block down on your right. Relax. You're fine."

"I can't. I'm about to take that AP exam."

Frank was good with details about his customers. That's why he was such a successful salesman, getting the teens to spend their birthday, Christmas money, and whatever they earned from part-time jobs, but this detail escaped him.

"You know, that test for advanced placement in college for English credit."

Like the pro he was, Frank quickly recovered. "Oh, yeah the one your brother Vince is always razzing you about."

"That too. My brother swears it was the most challenging test he ever took in his life and he was the class valedictorian of 1967. I'm no where near that but I've got to score well enough to pass that test."

"Hmm, that's pressure but knowing you, you'll do fine. Just focus on the moment, like you do when you play."

"Good advice Frank, thanks." Joe turned, walked to the door and opened it to the cacophony of a bustling Wabash Avenue. Joe yelled over the din, "If I choke, I'll never hear the end of it." He then disappeared into the crush of a sea of Chicagoans on his way to the dreaded AP exam.

* * *

The smell of petroleum and the buzz of machinery from six production lines greeted Beriso as he entered Anderson Inc. Operators pulled down and pushed up vats with spouts that pumped lighter fluid into cans of various sizes and labels that moved along a conveyor belt. Two employees on the crew at the end of the line finished off the process as one-capped cans while the other stored them into boxes piled on a pallet.

Elmer, the forklift operator ceased lifting a pallet when he caught the scent of the white bag. He turned to see the Chief walking toward the stairs leading to Dane's overhead office. With a whistle he caught the eye of Clarence and Melvyn looking over plans to revamp the warehouse layout. With a nod he got both men to follow Beriso's movement. Before climbing the black iron stairway, the three of them noticed the Chief stop to read an employee bulletin board.

"Clarence, do I smell beefs?" questioned Melvyn.

Clarence cocked his head back with his nose high in the air.

"Your sniffer is better than mine but yeah, it's beefs and the white bag fits. They're from Jimmy and Gina's."

"And what's with whitey's interest in our bulletin board?"

"Who knows Melvyn? You remember what's on it?"

"Nothing much. Just some safety-first notices and the announcement about the upcoming raffle for the two summer jobs."

The Chief turned from the board with a smile on his face and headed quickly up the black iron stairway to Dane's executive suite.

"Hmm. Maybe we'll find out, maybe we won't. But Melvyn, let's get back to your recommendations."

By seeking his one-time rival's opinion and advice on how to make the warehouse more efficient, Clarence healed a wound and converted an adversary to an ally. Even though he was dying to run upstairs to Dane's office and discover why the Chief was treating his boss to lunch, he had to focus on Melvyn's presentation. Something was up and Anderson, Inc.'s new foreman, still smarting from the whack he took the last time he saw the Chief, was sure it wasn't good.

* * *

Beriso reached Dane's outer office, where Lucille, a stylishly dressed, executively built stunning twenty-year-old mulatto sat typing. The big man in uniform startled her and it showed as one of her hands slipped off the keyboard causing her to make a mistake.

"Dammit, I'll have to start over."

The Chief stared, waiting to be recognized.

"May I help you?"

"Yeah, is your boss in?"

"Who may I say is calling?"

"I'll tell him for you." And with that the Chief walked through the door to the surprise and irritation of Dane, engaged in a phone conversation. He gave Beriso a slight nod, raised his right hand and with a slight wave bid the Chief to sit in one of two chairs before his massive cluttered dark oak desk.

"Trust me, we can fulfill Marshall Field's needs, meet the requirements of the contract and do it for less. We absolutely want your business. What more can I say?"

Dane listened intently and then nodded, "No problem. We can meet that deadline and be ready to start by next Monday."

The Chief watched with fascination as Dane, a master salesman plied his trade.

"That's great, Mr. Klazura! Thanks for the chance to prove we're as good if not better than Aquamatic Fluid Dispensers. Let me assure you that you and Marshall Fields have made the right choice. I'll send copies by messenger of a contract signed by me for your approval. You can return the contract to me in person. You pick the restaurant."

Dane nodded with a huge smile.

"Escargot? Why not!" Escargot was, as everyone knew in Chicago, a premiere, hard to get into and extremely expensive 5-star-restaurant.

Dane winced as he listened.

"The wives, sure, we'll make an evening of it."

Dane paused.

"Saturday at eight? No problem. I know the maître d'."

Dane's wince turned into a look of pure satisfaction.

"Okay, see you then. Good-bye."

Dane hung up the phone. He stood with a smile as he greeted the Chief with a strong firm handshake.

The Chief returned the gesture.

"So Chief, what brings you by?"

The Chief grabbed a beef from the bag and handed it to Dane.

"It's not Escargot but the beef will more than do for lunch. I understand you're one of Gina's best customers."

Dane laughed rubbing his belly.

"That's an understatement. I love these. Thanks."

Dane hit the intercom. "Lucille, bring us a couple of cold ones."

"Unlike some of my brethren, I don't drink on the job."

Dane smiled. "You don't drink Coca-Cola?"

"Oh, sure. I thought-"

The Chief stopped. He couldn't help but notice the wiggle of Lucille's sexy full figure as she served both men an eight-ounce bottle of icy cold Coca-Cola.

"Anything else Mr. Anderson?" said the lovely Lucille.

Dane smiled back at her. "Not for now. Thanks."

Dane continued to follow Lucille's exit out the door.

"I've never found Negroes attractive but that Lucille...well as you can see, she's something else."

The Chief snickered, "To each his own."

Both men took a bite from their sandwiches and a swig of their Cokes.

"So what can I do for you Chief? Is there a fireman's ball or something like that coming up?"

"Nah, we don't do those. That's strictly a cop thing."

The Chief ripped off another bite from his Italian beef. Dane followed suit digging into his tasty sandwich. Both men enjoyed the moment and the conversation seemed to be on hold.

Finally Dane broke the silence after downing another morsel of fresh baked Italian bread laden with juicy gravy well seasoned with herbs and spices.

"So to what do I owe this honor?"

John continued to chew before he delivered an answer. He would make Dane wait. This was chess at its finest. "Well, this is my district, and I do make it a point to know when fire inspectors from downtown invade my territory."

"So you know about the 12 violations?"

John nodded as he chewed.

"12 violations...typical for a place like this, huh Chief?"

"Yeah, but you've got a problem my friend."

Dane dug through a pile of papers on his desk. He found what he was looking for and held it up in his right hand.

"Here it is." Dane carefully scanned it. "Seven days? Hell, I don't know if I can get all these infractions fixed in that time frame." He looked up at the chief a bit miffed. "And what's with the $100 fine for everyday of noncompliance?"

John nodded. "Ever since the Our Lady of Angels fire, the city is overly cautious with public buildings."

The Our Lady of Angels parochial school fire claimed the lives of 92 children and three nuns on December 1, 1958.

.

It received national attention and sullied Chicago's reputation, and perpetuated the myth that the city that burned to the ground in 1871 was still an unsafe city when it came to fire. Chicago's Mayor Richard M. Daley, the political boss of Illinois, hated the press headlines and vowed that fire inspection and protection would not be compromised by graft, ineptitude or ignorance of the statutes.

John finished off his coke and placed it squarely on the front of Dane's desk with a bit of a bang. "100 bucks a day is a bit steep, but lucky for you, I can buy you some time."

"Oh, so you're here to rescue me Chief?

"Well, I-"

Dane slammed his coke bottle down on his side of the desk. "I know what this is and I don't like shakedowns Chief?"

John sneered. "I'm insulted Dane. I've never taken a bribe in my life. I just figured in this case we could help each other."

The taut lines in Dane's face and the veins in his neck relaxed. "Okay I'm listening. How can I help you?"

"My boys, Vince and Joe need summer jobs to help cover college expenses. But with the recession and the riots destroying Caputo's, the fruit and vegetable market where the boys have worked previously during their summer vacations...well...jobs are tight. That's where you come in."

"What's in it for me?"

"I can buy you thirty days without the fear of fines."

Dane's eyes lit up. "Now we're talking."

"But, you still have to fix everything Dane, and I mean everything."

"With your support and direction?"

The Chief removed his hat and wiped his brow. "Yeah, sure. So are we good?"

Dane put his hand to his chin and began to stroke it. "I've got a minor problem. We just instituted a raffle that will pick two kids from my employees via a drawing for summer work, the quarter when we're the busiest. It's a crowd pleaser, you know, employee morale and it brings us favor with Mayor Daley's summer youth jobs program. How about we make it one job. That way I'll be able to keep the peace."

"But you haven't had the drawing yet? Right?"

Dane nodded his head slightly as if to ask, "How the hell do you know?"

"No," Dane swigged a bit of Coke, "we haven't had the drawing yet?"

"Well then, we don't have a problem, do we? You're the owner, so who you hire is your business, right?" smiled the Chief. Since you're hiring two teenagers, you'll still be a hit with the Mayor's summer jobs program, right?"

Dane finished off the last morsel of sandwich. He crunched the wrapper into a ball and threw it into the basket. "Okay Chief, you got me at a disadvantage. Anderson's got to be on line or we lose a chance at that new business I just scored with Marshall Fields, besides having to lay employees off if we're shut down. To you," Dane nodded his head towards the windows revealing the activity of the plant, "they may be just a bunch of niggers but they got families too. That's what it's all about right, helping our families? You can empathize with that, yes?"

The Chief ingested the last morsel of his beef. "Delicious, yeah?" He refrained from looking at Dane concentrating on discarding the wrapper into the white bag he had brought from Gina's. His silence indicated that Dane would have to give him both jobs.

Dane sighed, "Okay, I'll set it up for your boys *this* summer but don't come knocking again. On June 1st have them report to Clarence, my foreman. He'll have to run interference for them."

"Interference? Why?" asked Beriso.

"Interference from employees who will be angry that I hired two white kids, brothers no less, not giving even one of their kids a shot at a summer job even though we made an announcement encouraging them to have their young submit applications."

The Chief shifted uncomfortably in his chair. He knew he'd crossed a line.

"But you don't have a problem with that, do you?" asked Dane.

The Chief nodded "No," but he couldn't help but notice a wry wee smile on Dane's face as he stood to leave. Like it or not, his boys would have to suck it up in a hostile setting. Dad had done the best he could do in the very rough year of 1968.

———

CHAPTER SIX

THE WILD DUCK

"Two minutes remaining," boomed the T.A. - teacher's assistant, a bearded ascetic academic, given the task of baby-sitting a lecture hall filled with high school seniors taking the National Advanced Placement (AP) Exam for English.

"Two minutes?" echoed exasperated examiners creating cleverly constructed composition capable of courting college credit recognition and the kudos that came with such an accomplishment.

Joe looked up and about when he caught the consternation of one of two monitors assisting the bearded academic in ensuring that no one cheated. Joe immediately rose to avert suspicion of cheating. He whisked the test papers off his armchair desk and headed toward the ascetic who thought of himself, literally and figuratively at the head of the class. "Young man, you realize you still have almost ninety seconds left."

"Ninety-seconds?" groaned a chorus of senior high school students, not nearly as comfortable with their progress as Joe seemed to be with his.

Joe submitted his test packet. "I'm done. Either I nailed it or I didn't."

"And what was that?"

Henrik Ibsen's, "The Wild Duck." replied Joe.

"You mean-"

Joe cut off the TA, not allowing him the pleasure of asserting his intelligence.

"Vildanden for those who can speak Norwegian. Do you?" asked a smart aleck Joe.

The aggrieved ascetic didn't respond to the question. Instead he insisted upon displaying his knowledge of the writer's work. "His 'Doll House' is better known."

"That's why I picked 'The Wild Duck,' considered by many to be his most complex if not finest work."

The bearded young man, only a few years older than Joe, laughed disdainfully at the cockiness of this high school senior before him. "All you need is a three but you presume to tackle a piece of work that grad students avoid. Why?"

"You wouldn't understand. In my home a three is not good enough."

The ascetic shook his head at Joe. He turned to a room full of struggling test-takers as he boomed, "Sixty-seconds." The echo of moans lamenting the fragility of time shook Joe as he entered the hallway forcing him to wonder if he had made a mistake. He'd know soon enough.

* * *

Dane created quite a stir within his factory when he opened the blinds in his office, slid open a large window with a bang followed by an angry scream, "Clarence, on the double, my office. NOW!"

Elmer shook by the outburst barely missed plowing into the Chief stepping off the iron wrought stairway as Clarence rushed past him. The Chief for a split second was caught in a flurry of movement and light from two different directions. A close encounter with Elmer and his forklift gave Beriso concern that developed into consternation for a culprit he viewed reckless. While continuing to negotiate a curve, Elmer turned back to catch Beriso's fiery eyes, part out of fear and part morbid curiosity. "Shit, that was close," Elmer realized, "I could have killed him, blinded by Clarence running the other way."

Factory workers on every line watched Clarence scale the top stairs to Dane's office. Anxiety filled their faces, as Clarence snapped to his master's voice. For some the image conjured ancestor anecdotal revelations about Uncle Toms and their need to curry the favor of the owner. It was as if their eyes could talk. You could see the look. "Why the hell did God give whitey all the fuckin' power?"

At that moment there wasn't a factory worker who didn't bond to Clarence. No matter what Jesus taught, not one of them would forgive Dane for humiliating "their" supervisor. He never treated Sullivan that way...at least not publicly in front of the entire plant.

Clarence slammed on the breaks just as he was about to hit the outer doorway of the Pullman. He looked through the window to luscious looking Lucille licking envelopes on behalf of the master. She in that buxom blouse smiled back at Clarence and beckoned him to come in.

Clarence grabbed the knob but couldn't get it to turn. That's when a buzzer sounded freeing the door to open. Clarence almost fell forward as he had to skip to keep his balance. He found himself in front of Lucille, who calmly proclaimed, "Dane's expecting you. Go on in. Good luck."

Clarence started for the door to Dane's office. He turned back at Lucille. "You know what he's upset about?"

Lucille stopped typing. She shook her head no.

"Damn! Even when he threatened to fire Elmer, he didn't sound that angry. Shit!" Clarence stopped. "Why the hell did he put a buzzer on that door?"

Lucille shrugged her shoulders to say, "Who knows?"

Clarence took a deep breath and then with a firm grip opened the door to Dane's lair. He held the door open as he made eye contact with Dane, seated behind a desk full of stuff piled on top of stuff. Dane saw the silhouette of a man, presumably Clarence, now back lit with the light that splashed through the windows of Lucille's part of the Pullman.

"Clarence, if that's you come in and shut the door."

As the door shut, the obnoxious back light faded to reveal a nervous foreman.

Clarence began to take a seat when Dane's look prompted him to stand.

"You see the fire chief that was just here?"

Clarence looked back to the door and remembered that the man he bounded by was indeed in uniform. The face appeared before him, blurred initially and then clearly forming into the face of the man with the fiery eyes.

"Sort of."

Dane handed Clarence a piece of paper.

"For your records. You'll need the Chief's information. I want you to hire his sons for the summer jobs."

"They're in addition to the drawing we're having, sir?"

"What drawing?"

"What drawing? Aw, c'mon boss, we talked about it. It's on all the bulletin boards. Remember, two kids for the summer line chosen from families of our own employees? You know, for morale."

Dane tilted his seat forward as he grabbed stuff off of stuff. "Well, there's been a change of plans." Dane took a pen to a work order, indicating new specifications necessary for the job. He didn't look at Clarence.

"C'mon boss, you're putting me between a rock and a hard place with the folks downstairs. They got excited about this. I'm sure the kids who get picked could really use the job, maybe for a shot at college."

Dane put the pen down. He peered at Clarence.

"Handle it. That's why you get more for being the foreman."

"But boss. There are flyers all over the plant."

"Which Lucille will take down after everyone leaves tonight. You've got the weekend to figure how to deal with the troops."

Clarence now understood where Lucille's loyalty lay. She knew.

"Look, if you can't handle it, I'll find somebody who can! Now get out of here! Can't you see I've got a ton of work to do."

Dane diddled with his papers. Clarence ambled to the door, upset, but smart enough to keep his mouth shut.

"And remember Clarence. As to the Chief's boys," Dane pointed at his charge, intent on seizing his attention, "Not so much as a hair off their heads...or it's off with your head. Are we perfectly clear?"

Clarence nodded, turned and exited the office. He was surprised to find Cederick, Melvyn and Frederick waiting for him at the bottom of the black iron stairwell.

"What'd he get you for?" asked Cederick.

Before he had a chance to answer, Frederick piped in, "Caught you with your hand in the till, huh?"

Clarence smirked at the implication, set to pounce when Melvyn spurt out in laughter, "He give you the boot?"

It was the laugh. Had he not said it with the laugh, it would have been okay. But that damn laugh triggered an explosion. "Dumb ass wise guys! Think you're funny? Get your butts back to work unless you want the boot! Now get!"

The men scattered. Clarence's wrath shook throughout the plant as some sheepishly stole glances at a foreman who now seemed so foreign.

"Give me the boot?" mumbled Clarence as he shared a dagger of a look with each of the onlookers. This time they all heard what had only been a mumble. "Give me the boot? Not if I have anything to say about it."

* * *

The Wilson kitchen table served as court for a home-cooked meal that included crispy fried chicken, collared greens, corn bread, mash potatoes and sassy sweet potato pie. Clarence picked at his food as he stared out the window at a backyard tableau that featured his children, Hailey and Junior, squealing with delight as their Grandma pushed them up and away towards a crescent moon in a crimson twilight sky turning midnight blue.

Jackie, consumed with cleaning the dishes, the counters, and the stove after serving quite the meal, failed to recognize Clarence's funk; he was awash in a world of his making. It was only when she gathered the leftovers that she noticed her man was lost and far, far away.

"What's troubling you sugar? Come to think of it, you didn't say a word to the kids at dinner."

"Nothing."

"Right." Jackie's head tilted to her right as her left eyebrow rose up in disbelief.

"Aw nuts." Clarence, pissed for weakening, let it out. "It's not fair."

"What's not fair?"

"I've got to hire two white boys for those summer jobs."

"Why would two white boys want to work in a factory full of black folk?" Jackie snickered with a slight "huh" at the bottom of her breath.

"I hope they don't. But that's not what I'm facing. Dane's making me hire the local fire chief's sons and I'm damned if I do and damned if I don't."

"Wait, are the white boys in addition to the drawing?"

Clarence sharply responded, "No!"

"Okay, I can see you're stressed. That's a predicament. But I'm sure you can convince Dane to keep his word."

Clarence looked at her, astonished.

Jackie was compelled to ask, "So, you gave Dane a piece of your mind?"

Clarence's head slid back like a bobble doll. "Are you out of your mind? If I'd done that, I'd be the one looking for a summer job."

Jackie's face filled with incredible astonishment challenged Clarence. "You're not letting this slide are you?"

"Damn right I am. You like this house? You want the kids to attend public school or stay in the parochial one? And the car, and the pretty dresses, you like those?"

"Yeah, I like to wear 'em but I tell you this Clarence. I was happy before you became foreman. If the price is that high, and you can't keep your word, than I'll get a job. But to buckle to Dane's failure to keep a promise, that's not the man I married."

"Yeah it is. It's rough out there. I'm the man of this house. I'm the one responsible not only to you, but the kids, my mother and myself. I didn't come this far to see it all disappear."

Jackie shook her head. She looked at Clarence in shock. "I never thought you'd sell-

Clarence grabbed his wife tight to him. "Jackie, I'm not selling out. I'm no Uncle Tom so don't go there. I get enough of that shit at work. But what nobody gets, and obviously not even you...I'm breaking ground just like Jackie Robinson, maybe not as celebrated because I'm just a working stiff, but what I'm doing is just as important...not just for me but for others that follow. So that any man, even a colored man, can be a foreman, a manager or yes even someday, maybe an owner of a factory. But if I can't follow orders, that ain't going to be..."

Jackie put her sweet lips to his. "I got it." She kissed him over and over to tell him, without saying it, how sorry, how very, very sorry she was to question his integrity. She led him by the hand to their bedroom, shut the door and locked it.

Tonight, grandma would put the kids to bed.

—

CHAPTER SEVEN

THE CLASS OF 1968

The weekend arrived. Clarence planned to sleep in but that dream disappeared as he and Jackie, out of duty to Faye, attended the Hyde Park Academy graduation ceremony. Faye's son, Lawrence, had the honorable distinction of being the class valedictorian and the duty of delivering an inspiring address to his classmates for that honor.

"We've been witness to so much already in 1968; the assassination of Dr. King, the violent aftermath in our streets here in Chicago and cities nationwide. On top of everything else, the war and a recession are having an impact on our economy that has unjust consequences to black America. A draft that targets the poor, thus forcing black Americans to serve in Vietnam in record numbers compared to previous wars. As bleak as this sounds, I prefer to keep close to my heart a hope for all of you, deeply rooted in the American experience. To quote Dr. King, 'I have a dream that one day this nation will rise up and live out the true meaning of its creed.'"

Lawrence paused. He scanned the eyes of the entire class of graduates.

"You have the arduous task of breaking barriers and setting standards of excellence. You have a duty, an obligation to not only raise yourself up, but that of others. I pray. as I know you do, that Dr. King's life and death will not go in vain. It may be tough, it's going to be rough, but with God's help we shall overcome. Thank you!"

The audience rose and gave Lawrence a resounding standing ovation. Jackie and Clarence both smiled their approval to Faye who was beaming and welling up with tears of pride and joy.

Lawrence bowed to the audience as the principal approached the podium. He shook hands with Lawrence as he addressed the students. "The class of 1968 is officially dismissed."

The caps floated up and away as the class of 1968 went wild. It was good to be young.

* * *

After the hoopla, Faye, Jackie and Clarence greeted Lawrence in the hallway with hugs from the women and a firm handshake from Clarence.

Faye squealed with delight, "My boy. My God, you made me proud." She turned to the Wilson's. "Wasn't he something?"

"Sure was." Jackie smiled. "That was a beautiful speech, Lawrence."

Lawrence blushed. "Thank you Mrs. Wilson."

"He's going to make a great attorney someday. You watch and see Clarence."

Clarence smiled at the young man. "I can already see it. You're quite the orator, son." Clarence put his hand to his chin in amazement. "An attorney, now that is something I'd love to see."

Faye put her arm around her son and squeezed. "I hope you're all headed to my place. I'm serving barbeque." Faye noticed Jackie's look at Clarence. She didn't want to press but she did. "Please say you'll come."

Clarence smiled at Faye. "We'd love to but I've got a wake to go to and Jackie's got to relieve Mama whose made plans to play Bingo tonight with her friends."

Jackie wanted to nip it in the bud. "You know Clarence's mama ain't willing to miss her Bingo night."

Faye, resigned to Jackie's "No," saw an opening to address what she really wanted to discuss. "Well you can make it up to me."

Clarence was puzzled. "How?"

Jackie was intrigued as well and waited for the answer when Lawrence asked her to take a picture of him with some of his classmates. Jackie couldn't refuse and found her straining to hear the answer as she clicked away.

Faye felt a tad uncomfortable and pulled Clarence aside to share her answer only with him. "You know I wouldn't ask this, but it's for my Lawrence. Even though he's got a scholarship, we don't have enough money to enroll him in a full time schedule."

Clarence empathized with Faye's concern. Less than a full time schedule at school could lead one to lose their deferment from the draft resulting in conscription to the horrors of Vietnam. "Gee Faye, I don't know how much I can spare but I'll talk it-

Faye cut him off. "I'm not asking for your charity."

Clarence was ruffled by the abruptness.

"All I want is for you, as foreman, to make sure my Lawrence is one of the two names pulled from the upcoming drawing. If he's not a full-time student, you know the danger he faces. He's a deserving boy who will make us all proud."

Jackie, returned to the adults, after taking a photo with Lawrence.

"You would really want me to fix it?" asked Clarence.

Faye, conscious of Jackie's presence found it uncomfortable to say her peace, but she was a determined mother protecting her young. "I don't care if it's wrong. I want you to fix it. Lawrence deserves it. He's got promise. You can see that. I don't want my baby to be wasted in some rice paddy, for what, for whom. It ain't fair, he's worked too hard to fail."

Clarence couldn't find fault with Faye even if he found it with himself. He didn't have the heart, or maybe it was the guts, to tell Faye that a drawing wasn't even on the board. "Faye, I'll do whatever it takes to make sure Lawrence doesn't wind up in that situation. Let me see what I can do."

Faye realized Clarence couldn't say it out loud, but she knew from his look that her son would be safe. "Best doggone thing Dane ever done in the fifteen years I've been there, and I know you had a lot to do with the drawing. Thank you."

Clarence nodded in agreement, as he squirmed with guilt, something only a wife, confidant or a lover could surmise. Jackie wondered how a good man like her husband, could risk disappointing Lawrence and hurting Faye. Truth, no matter how it sets you free, at times enslaves you when it endangers the dreams of a deserving young man breaking ground. That was something Clarence could relate to firsthand.

* * *

Vince exited Charlie's '60 hot-red Pontiac Catalina. It was good to be home for the summer. Charlie emptied his trunk of Vince's luggage.

John, dressed in a cook's apron left the spit of the barbecue grill to welcome home his oldest son.

"Vince, how's my boy?" John gave his son a bear hug. "C'mon, we're just about set to eat. Hungry?"

"You bet dad."

"Charlie, thanks for picking him up from the station. There's a cold Falstaff in the cooler with your name on it."

Charlie smiled as the three men walked to a back yard filled with family and friends. A banner attached to the garage read, "CONGRATULATIONS GRADUATE." At the sight of Vince, Gloria jumped from her seat to embrace her first born. Joe followed.

"You're home son!" Gloria enclosed her boy in her arms.

"Finally. Champagne to Chicago is a long ride." Vince extended his hand to Joe. "Hey there bro. Congratulations on finishing St. Pat's, you did it! Where'd you wind up?" Vince smiled as he awaited an answer.

Joe smiled but deliberately refused to answer Vince's query as he turned to Charlie. "Charlie, give me the bags, I'll take care of them. Even though it's my big day, the first-born son has returned and that's not something we can ignore."

Charlie handed the bags over as he looked into the eyes of both young men. "You two are sure funny, in a weird sort of way. Must be from your mom's side because it sure ain't from your old man." Charlie winked. "I'd know."

Joe's eyes twinkled at the observation. Charlie had a knack for lighting up Joe's face. Joe took the bags up to their shared room.

Joe returned to a table filled with barbecue, roasted corn, pasta, baked potatoes with green beans smothered in olive oil and Italian bread. Gloria poured ice tea for each guest. Joe took his seat next to Vince who sat next to their mother. Gloria sat next to John who always occupied the seat at the head of the table. Gloria had John to her left and her boys to her right. To John's left sat Charlie McGann. The rest of the table was filled with cousins, aunts and uncles, grandmas and one grandpa. John rose to propose a toast. He held up his Pabst Blue Ribbon. "To Joe, our graduate, who did it with honors, and also to a fine year of good grades by our college boy, Vince. Good going men. Your mother, the family and your father are proud of your hard work; you are the first men from this family to attain college status."

From the table came a chorus of "Salute" as glasses or bottles clinked.

"So, in appreciation for a job well-done, I thought I'd give your mother the day off from a hot stove while I whipped up some barbecue."

Vince leaned over to his brother. "Thank God he cooked."

Joe nodded in agreement. There was no question that big John was the chef even if Mom was the chief at home. They loved their mother but her cooking at times was awful.

"So dig in everyone. Enjoy." John sat down.

Trays of food moved about the table as family and friends shared food and conversation.

John turned to face Gloria, Vince and Joe.

"Good news. I got you boys jobs for the summer."

"That's great dad!" Vince bit into another rib.

Joe needed to know more. "Where?"

"Joe, you ask too many questions. We'll talk about it later."

"John, our youngest asked a legitimate question." Gloria continued, "Besides, I want to know where my sons are working as well, so spill it."

John took a swig of his Pabst and savored the taste before he "spilled" the unsavory details. "At a factory in my district."

"Oh my God, John. That's the heart of the riot area!"

"I know Gloria. I work there, tell me about it."

"I don't believe this." Gloria ripped her napkin off her lap and placed it firmly on the table as she looked to John for some comfort.

"What's the problem? The boys will ride with me to work."

"And when you're on for 24, how do they get home?"

Vince, Joe and Charlie watched and waited. They knew better than interrupt when John and Gloria were at it.

"They'll take the streetcar."

"I don't like the sound of that. John, you work in a rough neighborhood."

"Yeah but even Charlie will tell you, things are calming down. Right, Charlie?"

Charlie didn't miss a beat. Here was his cue to enter the fray and come to the rescue. "Gloria, trust us. You have nothing to worry about."

John placed his hand on his wife's.

"See. Charlie can back me up. Besides, the owner's assigned a guy to look after them. The foreman."

"And who's that?" Gloria waited. "You don't know his name?"

"Yeah, it's a, ah...Clarence.   That's it.   Clarence Wilson."

"That sounds like a colored name." She stared at John.

"Well what if it is? It's an all black factory, but the guy who owns it is white."

"What?" Gloria was flushed in the face.

"Well, they can't go back to Caputo's Market, Gloria. It burned down and they're not reopening for some time."

Both parents fell silent. They ate as they avoided eye contact. The boys realized it was their cue to say something reassuring to their mother.

"Mom, it'll be okay." Vince offered. "Besides, we need jobs. Joe and I've got to have money of our own down at U of I."

Gloria slowly turned her head to look at her sons.

"Yeah mom, if that's what dad wants," volunteered Joe.

Pissed, she cut Joe off. "Don't tell me how to talk to your father. He's the one who's always spouting how they're nothing but animals. Now he wants to send you boys into that lion's den?"

"C'mon Gloria. I busted my ass to get them jobs."

Gloria shook her head. "What was I thinking? I should have known. You cut a deal. It's always a little shady, isn't it?"

Charlie tried his best to keep a straight face but couldn't help but break a wry smile. The Chief's old lady was chewing out his boss. Moments like these were priceless.

John decided to change the subject. "So Mr. Big Man on Campus, what's it like?"

Vince put down a rib and wiped his face with a napkin. Why did mom let him shift the spotlight from father to son? "It's intense and intuitive."

"In-toot-ti-tive?"

"Pop, it's pronounced IN-TU-I-TIVE."

John bristled at the correction. "C'mon speak English."

"I am," protested Vince, "but nah, you don't get it even when I do."

Gloria tried to check her son's sarcasm. "Vince, that's no way to talk to your father."

"What? I can't use vocabulary acquired at college?"

"Not if it means belittling someone." Gloria served as a compass for good no matter which of her men needed straightening.

Uncle Steve sat next to Charlie. He had been talking to cousins but found the conversation of John's immediate family much more interesting. He decided to join in. "Just because your old man didn't finish the ninth grade doesn't mean he's as dumb as he looks."

"I'll take that as a compliment Uncle Steve." John reached across Charlie and clinked beer bottles with his uncle.

Joe hated when Vince acted like a know-it-all. "You could have used *thought provoking* rather than intuitive."

Big John liked that. "Now that I can understand."

Vince was miffed at his brother for making him look pompous. "Okay, I'll try and speak at your level."

Joe resented the implied put-down. "And when you do talk at our level, please avoid using 'nah' and 'don't' in the same sentence. It's confusing because it's a double negative."

Uncle Steve laughed. "Hmm, So much for the big investment."

———

"When a father gives to his son, both laugh;
When a son gives to his father, both cry."
-William Shakespeare

CHAPTER EIGHT

FAMILY FIRST

A line of white duct tape ran on the floor from the doorway to the opposite wall with windows. The division of lifestyles was obvious even without the divider. One side of the room featured sports memorabilia and trophies. A collage of musical posters and album art covered the walls of the other side. A Formica steer's head, secured to the awning that covered the curtain rod assembly, overlooked the room. It was completely out of place but something John had bought as a decoration for the room, and so a place was found for it. The boys used the hollowed out head to stash everything from cigarettes to the headset of a phone that had a dial taped to the body with electrical tape. There was also an illegitimate phone connection tucked into that steer's head that surreptitiously ran up to the roof and then down to the telephone exchange box in the basement. If the boys had to make a call without their parents knowing it, they could.

Joe, sat up in his bed, propped against a pillow as he read Billboard Magazine. Vince unpacked open luggage sitting on his bed. He transferred his clothes to a small dresser that sat on his side of the room. A matching dresser mirrored it on Joe's side.

Joe put his magazine down. He was itching to say something.

Vince returned to the luggage when he caught a look from Joe. "What's up?"

"Why'd you have to call Pop out like that?"

"What?" Vince sat on the edge of the bed next to bags that had been emptied. "He knows how to give it. So, once in a while, he ought to take it."

"Not in front of family. A father merits more than that."

"You didn't seem to have a problem correcting me."

"You deserved it for trying to make dad look like an idiot."

"Idiot? You're the idiot for considering a career in music."

"Change the subject, huh? Okay, I'll bite. What's so terrible Vince, about me being a musician?"

"To start, zero security, misfits, longhaired hippies and freaky people."

"A lot of those misfits are millionaires."

"And you're going to be one of 'em? That's a one-in-a-million shot. You'd be better off going to law school."

"I remember when you burned to play for the Yankees. You had the goods. You hit 330 in your junior year. Scouts were looking at you. You had a chance."

"I blew my knee."

"Vince, you had it fixed. You played after that. Be honest, you're playing it safe."

Vince arose and slid over to his bags turning his back to his brother. "Maybe. But being a doctor will get me the money and prestige I want out of life. More than Pop's got."

"Yeah, but he loves what he's doing."

Joe heard Vince grunt a "huh" followed by a chuckle.

From under a pile of clothes, Vince pulled out a box. He turned, stepped over the divide and offered it to his brother. "Got you a gift for graduating."

"Wow. Far out!"

The box was wrapped in newspaper comics. Joe ripped off the paper. "A Rogers? A Rogers drum pedal? How'd you get it? You just got home."

"Uncle Steve was kind enough to pick it up for me, but I paid for it."

"This is the best! Thanks Vince!"

"Yeah. Aside from how I feel about...well, you're my brother and I know you wanted one. So be happy."

Joe flashed Vince a smile that quickly changed. "Now get on your side of the room!" shouted Joe.

Vince surprised, then delighted by the shout, grabbed Joe's head in a headlock and polished the pate of his noggin. They had differences but they were brothers, no mistake about it; and yet they were so much more. That's why they could always end as friends; friends who greet each other with a smile that says, "I love you even when you're a pain in the ass." After all, they were family.

* * *

The Hope Baptist Church glistened a cocoa-colored red as the Sun's rays blossomed and refracted light to set the brownstone aglow. The joy of a choir could be heard wailing, "How I Got Over," the prayer made famous by Aretha Franklin, the artist, dubbed by WVON disc jockey, Pervis Spann, as the "Queen of Soul." Spann had won national notoriety with his 87-hour sleepless sit-in to raise money for Dr. Martin Luther King.

In the congregation sat Clarence, dressed in a marine military suit, along with his family, Faye and her son Lawrence.

Reverend Clemmons rose from a chair in an ornate sanctuary. The choir finished with bravado just as Clemmons arrived at the podium. He looked out on a congregation that had just experienced the ecstasy of a soul-full choir performance.

Then the quiet ensued for a good five seconds - an eternity before the Reverend Clemmons thundered. "I got over! I got over! Hallelujah. Oh, thank you Jesus. Brothas and sistas, I feel the Holy Spirit whipping through this congregation, like the wind. How we got over?"

Then the whisper..."That's what we're talking about today, this Memorial Day when we honor those who've sacrificed for God and country."

Then plain speaking..."So what do we need to do, to get through these tough times? The Lord says, in Psalms 10:17, 'Lord, thou has heard the desire of the humble: thou wilt prepare their heart, thou wilt cause thine ear to hear.'"

Reverend Clemmons had the attention of every soul in the Lord's House, Hope Baptist Church. "God will answer if you look unto him."

Clemmons looked out to his flock and they looked unto him, a father, a minister, a friend...family.

"Now before I get started, there are a few announcements I want to make. Sista Samantha Clark and Brotha Lou Bennett are organizing a can food drive for families displaced by the riots."

Clarence awoke from the trance of Reverend Clemmons as the drone of his voice became background music for his thoughts. "Damn, I can't get away from those riots. I work in the heart of them." He looked at his lovely wife and children and wondered if they truly appreciated the challenge he faced day-in-and-day-out working in that neighborhood. Clarence lived with the fear, the anxiety that comes with a daily reminder that black people can and at times do turn on other black folk. It wasn't just the white man you had to fear, it was everybody and anybody. For a brief moment Clarence resented them, the ones he loved most in his life, because they had no clue of his sacrifice, partly because he didn't want them to understand, to do so would have made him hurt even more.

Slowly the words of the Reverend brought Clarence back in sync with the rest of the congregation.

"Brotha Kenny Blakely departed us in the most horrific way known to man, war. So we're going to pray for Sista Betty, Kenny's mother, a tireless worker on behalf of this community. We're going to pray unto the Lord for Sista Betty and all the rest of those who are in battle and those being drafted to war so that they can *get over*. These are tough times, your hearts are in pain, your minds are in rage, your fists are clinched, but brothas and sistas, the time will pass and bring a new day. The book of Ecclesiastes 3:3, God says there's, 'A time to kill, and a time to heal; a time to break down, and a time to build up, a time to mourn, and a time to dance.' Congregation, that day will soon come. Just put your faith in the Almighty and you will *get over*."

Clarence looked up as a stream of sunshine poured through a stain glass window. The light rested on his wife and children, now looking lovelier in the radiance. "I hear you Jesus," echoed in his mind. He knew it wasn't a coincidence, it was the Lord and Clarence Wilson in a language that was more complete without the encumbrance of words. Clarence had to do more than just be. He had to lead; to set an example. When the Lord calls, you don't say, "No."

———

"With America's sons in the fields far away, with America's future under challenge right here at home, with our hopes and the world's hopes for peace in the balance every day, I do not believe that I should devote an hour or a day of my time to any personal partisan causes or to any duties other than the awesome duties of this office--the Presidency of your country. Accordingly, I shall not seek, and I will not accept, the nomination of my party for another term as your President."

Lyndon B. Johnson
36th President of the United States–
March 31, 1968

"Caution: Being a Marine in Khe Sahn may be hazardous to your health."

U.S. Marine
3rd BN 26th - 1968
(quote on his flak jacket as captured by Newsweek photographer).

CHAPTER NINE

WE DON'T NEED ANOTHER KENNY

The Reverend ended each service with a blessing that encompassed all. He then moved down the center aisle bestowing his blessing to the right and then the left. At the very end of the center aisle was the vestibule where the "Rev" would wait to shake the hand of every sinner exiting the church. "But that's okay if you're a sinner brothas and sistas, because God loves the sinner," so says God and the Rev.

"Ah," smiled a peaceful Rev. "It's always a blessing to see the lovely Wilson family," a phrase repeated each Sunday.

Diedre blushed and each week answered for the family, "Why thank you, Reverend Clemmons.

Jackie would then smile with sincerity and add, "It was a beautiful sermon."

The ritual was on and if there is one thing that you can always count on when it comes to the church - no matter the denomination - it's tradition.

"Why thank you, Sista Jackie. And you Sista Diedre get younger every time I see you."

Clarence winced at witnessing his mother's orgasmic delight at hearing the tenor of the Rev's deep baritone voice make the inane compliment. Diedre craved that one moment every Sunday morning the way a spider yearns to build a web. She missed the touch of her husband, a sweet, gentle kind man who shared his life with her and the raising of their only son, Clarence. Diedre was proud of her son and thus proud of her husband, for it was his example of what it meant to be a good man that her son attempted to emulate.

"Oh stop that!" Diedre shouted in laughter. Then the smile would flash between Diedre and the Rev.

Jackie could see that her husband never noticed their true connection. Men don't notice other men when they cheat. But Jackie knew...she knew by the look. Only a man who has been intimate with a woman looks at a woman the way the Reverend looked at Diedre, or so Jackie thought.

"Thank y'all for coming."

And that's where the ritual would end, but not today. Clarence commanded the kids and the adults to give him the privacy that the man of the house rarely demanded. "Give me a second with the Reverend." Clarence handed Jackie the keys. "Kids, go with your Mom and Grandma."

Jackie and Diedre acquiesced by ushering the unwilling kids to the car.

Other parishioners sauntered by both men respectful that the pastor was engaged. To be engaged with the pastor usually meant there were "problems" in your life. Sometimes the issues were small but nine times out of ten they were heavy. Besides the fact that the routine had been broken, was an uncomfortable site for Diedre and Jackie, both wondering why Clarence needed the privacy. "Families on course don't break the routine!"

Clarence looked down.

"What's troubling you son?"

"It's one of my workers. You know, Faye."

"Sista Harris? Of course! Her son made a memorable graduation speech, didn't he?"

"Yeah, that's what I wanted to talk with you about. Unless Lawrence can find work this summer, he's not going to be able to afford college."

"Oh, that's not good." The minister brushed his brow. "He needs to be full-time, otherwise he could find himself drafted."

"Yeah, we don't want another Kenny."

"The Lord wants all his children to reach their potential." Reverend Clemmons looked hard and long at Clarence. "Can't you find him something down at the factory?"

"Pastor, I haven't had the heart to tell Faye that I can't, that's why I'm asking for your help."

Reverend Clemmons saw in Clarence what he had seen in his father, compassion.

"Let me think on this a day or two, Clarence. I'll get back to you."

Clarence extended his hand and shared a heartfelt handshake with a mentor that reminded him of his father. He was truly blessed.

* * *

John Beriso liked the look of his uniform. He had wanted to fight in World War II but his job as a trained professional fire fighter prevented that from happening. The homeland required seasoned firemen. London was bombed incessantly. The fear was that it could happen in the U.S. or so the military chiefs professed. And who would consider arguing with them? If Lieutenant Coronel Jimmy Doolittle could lead a squad to bomb a completely surprised Tokyo, only four months after Pearl Harbor, anything was possible by an enemy.

John looked into the room across the hall to see Gloria primp the hair of each of her boys. Vince allowed her one pass and then lost his patience.

"Knock it off, Ma."

Gloria turned to Joe to do the same.

Joe gingerly responded. "Mommm, I got it."

"Oh c'mon. I just want you boys to make a nice impression."

"For cryin' out loud Glor, it's a factory. They'll wind up in coveralls, so forget it."

Gloria more hurt than mad. "They're still my babies."

John had enough. "In the car now!" Vince and Joe moved.

John shook his head at Gloria, turned and walked out.

Next door to the north, the precinct captain, Danny Begley waved to John as he exited the Beriso home, ready to join the boys in the Bel-Air. John waved back. Beriso noticed that his neighbor, Stella, was upset with Begley. "She's pissed" thought John, "that somebody finked on her to the ward boss." John's mind continued to wind, "She probably thinks it's me. Damn, I wish it had been."

John waved to Stella but she ignored the fireman and his boys as they drove away. John could see in the rear view mirror, that Danny Begley was animated; he was probably laying down the law, which everyone on the block had heard at least once. "If the alderman hears about an infraction, he sends me out, and you gotta comply." In Chicago, if you knew what was good for you, you did what you were told by the precinct captains, who did what they were told by the ward bosses who complied with the wishes and dictates of his honor, Richard M. Daley. It was that simple.

* * *

For Vince and Joe, the ride opened their eyes. Seeing the destruction on TV didn't compare to witnessing it firsthand. Chicago's west side looked like Hiroshima after the blast.

John pulled the Bel-Air onto the apron of the factory's driveway. Oversized closed coppery-brown double bi-fold doors greeted them as they approached a proscenium arch that had sculpted into the grey brick stone at the top, "Anderson, Inc." To their left, as you looked at the building, was a burnished colored door marked, "Entrance." As they exited the car, two factory workers pushed opened the bi-fold doors.

John threw the gear into park. The boys exited the car but before moving an inch towards Anderson, they turned back to their father and gave him their undivided attention as they stood by the open front passenger window. "Guys, I don't want any flack from your mother, so work with me. Do as you're told and stick together."

Vince and Joe nodded and delivered in brotherly unison, "Okay Pop."

"Now, Clarence, is your guy. Find him boys and report to him." John drew his boys in tight to the window of the car with nothing but a look followed by the choice words, "But remember this!" The boys strained to listen as their father whispered, "Never, and I mean never, ever trust a nigger! Never, understand?" A look passed between the generations; from father to sons; some things were accepted without question.

The boys, with lunch bags in hand, turned away from the Bel-Air as they ambled forward to the tactile excitement of a new job, filled with new sounds, new sights and the pungent smell of petrochemicals.

As John drove off he watched his sons from his rear view mirror disappear into Anderson, as he wondered aloud, "What the fuck was I thinking? God, please keep my boys safe."

* * *

Vince and Joe walked through the huge gateway into a factory filled with workers jovially jostling one another as they took to their workstations. One by one Anderson employees caught sight of the intruders who appeared as if they belonged.

Vince and Joe felt the cold hard stares.

Out of the nowhere of an awkward moment stepped a tall thin black man. Vince talked first. He was the oldest. It was ritual.

"We're looking for Mr. Wilson."

"That would be me. And you must be, the Beriso brothers, our summer employees?"

"What did he say?" could be seen on every black face within hearing distance of Clarence. "Say it isn't so," could then be seen in the eyes of the listeners.

"Yeah, I'm Joe and this is my older brother, Vince." The younger sibling broke the ritual.

Clarence extended his hand for a shake. "Pleasure to meet you boys." The boys hesitated for a beat and then shook hands with Clarence.

Woodrow, a line operator, 6 feet 7 inches tall with a gaunt face, was setting up a machine when the Beriso brothers walked in. He hadn't notice what had just transpired. "Them boys lost Clarence?"

Clarence scanned his brain for the most diplomatic and deferential answer. Woodrow had been at the plant forever.

"Nobody's lost Wood. They're supposed to be here."

One-by-one, small eruptions blasted queries: "Supposed to be here?" "What?" "Since when..."What are you talking about Clarence?"

Clarence paid no mind to the comments. He focused on the boys. "Over there's the locker room. You'll find your names on a couple of lockers. Put on the overalls. It get's dirty around here."

Clarence noticed the lunch bags. "You need to refrigerate those bags?"

The boys shook their head no. Vince responded, "It's just PB&J with an apple, so we're good."

Factory workers parted like the Red Sea as Vince and Joe walked to the locker room. That parting quickly came together as workers closed around Clarence.

Jeffrey, a twenty-two year old with Hollywood looks, said what everyone was thinking. "What's with letting them two in here?"

Faye didn't care one way or another as long as there was a job for her Lawrence. But Faye was curious to be sure. "You puttin' four on for the summer?"

Kenny, a maintenance set-up man with an attractive smile, fit physique and handsome salary, was confused by the boys' arrival. He had started at Anderson on the same day as Clarence. He pressed the foreman as to what was going on. "What's up bro? When's the big drawing?"

Silence forced more eruptions.

"Yeah, when is it Clarence?" "Yeah, Clarence, when?" "C'mon man, don't be holding out on us."

Clarence surveyed the eyes. They were not to be denied.

"There's not gonna be a drawing."

Faye couldn't believe it. "There's not going to be a drawing? Since when?"

Eruptions were followed by more outbursts. "My kid was countin' on that shot...So was mine...But damn our kids don't even get a shot? How long you known about this? It ain't fair Massa Foreman that those two white boys got those jobs!"

The last reference with the "Stepin Fetchit" lilt burned a hole in Clarence's heart. Most whites loved watching Stepin Fetchit, an actor who portrayed the lazy and dumb Negro. The actual actor, Lincoln Theodore Monroe was anything but dumb and had the rare distinction of being the first black actor to become a millionaire for his thespian talents.

Clarence responded curtly, "It's not my call! It's not my call!"

Faye flashed, "What do you mean it's not your call? You're the damn foreman, ain't you?"

Kenny, a Clarence ally, repeated the foreman's assertion, "You hear the man, it ain't his call."

Kenny's allegiance caught the full flash of Faye's fury. "You playin' the puppet to the boss so you can keep that set-up job and the dough that comes with it?"

Eruptions spewed. "You nothing but a Tom, is you? Shit, you sold us out Wilson... ya damn porch monkey...nothing but a house nigga!"

Clarence laughed at the last one. That was it. That was the straw. He was the fucking foreman and he didn't have to answer to any of them. So it burned inside his brain even if he didn't verbalize it, "Fuck 'em. They niggas too!"

———

CHAPTER TEN

WETBACK

In the locker room at the plant, Joe was zipping into his coveralls as Vince, already dressed, sat on a bench, tying his shoes. Spanish singing slivered from a stall. The tone was soft with heart, almost like a whistle and sadly misunderstood. The boys looked at one another and then both turned their focus to the stalls. The boys moved closer. They saw Diego mopping up a disaster that reeked with stink. Diego smiled at Joe and Vince, as they winced from the foul odor.

Joe turned his wince to smile. "Hi there."

Diego smiled and nodded.

"What's your name? Ah...Como se llama?" Vince loved to show off. He knew enough Spanish to fool the family into thinking he was bilingual; he felt compelled to continue the charade. After school he worked on perfecting the language, and other skills, with a Mexican co-ed that he hid from everyone. That fact he sure as hell kept to himself.

Diego, a short Cuban janitor around 40 or so, decided to have some fun with the white boys.

"No speek-a-Englese."

"That's why I said it in Spanish. 'Como se llama?'"

"Oh, mi nombre, my name?" The Cuban winked at Joe. "Mi... wetback."

Joe and Vince both burst into laughter.

Diego laughed with them. When they all seemed to recover, Diego gave them his name. "Mi nombre es Diego Maria Rivera de Baz."

Joe looked to Vince for a translation.

"He says his name is Diego Maria Rivera Baz. The Negroes got him thinking his name in English is wetback. But my guess is he knows better." Diego smiled. Vince wondered if Diego was a lot smarter than he looked.

"Look at the filth they left." Joe conjectured, "they had to aim to miss that far."

"Holy shit," Vince spit, "what do you think we're in for if that's what they do to the brown man."

Joe didn't want to think of that. He just wanted the fucking spending money he needed to get through a year of school. He was part of a family intent on improving with each generation. Joe was bound and determined to do whatever it took to fulfill that expectation.

* * *

Dane followed the confrontation from his executive suite in the sky. He knew that Clarence was going to take heat from the employees. "Ah, better him than me." Dane wasn't sure how he'd react to insults from employees. He'd probably fire them, and they all seemed to know that. But with the killing of King, he didn't know what to expect. Lately, they were getting pretty uppity. Dane knew it was just a matter of time before someone would challenge even him and he felt guilty for sticking it to Clarence.

Dane decided to leave the safety of his office. He moved down the stairs and stood next to his foreman. The bitching stopped. The timing was picture perfect as Vince and

Joe exited the locker room. Dane asked Clarence, "Are those the Chief's sons?"

"In the flesh sir," replied a deferential Clarence.

That's all Dane needed to know as he moved forward to greet the boys with a, "Welcome to Anderson, Inc., where we fill any fluid from 3-in-1 oil to Kerosene."

Faye moved into position as operator of her line, but continued to monitor the drama unfolding before her. Dane waved good-bye as he headed back to his Pullman car in the sky. It was clear. "Fuck with my good friends and you're done."

Workers began to bow their head. The Massa had spoken. "Bullshit!" Faye fumed.

Clarence walking with the boys took them to the 3-in-1-oil production line. He pointed out their tasks. "You, Joe, will screw caps on filled containers. Vince, you'll load 'em into the corrugated boxes." Clarence motioned with his eyes first to get them to look across the way at another production line across the aisle. "See how they do it? Simple huh?" smiled Clarence to the boys.

Vince and Joe both looked yonder. Their look was met with hard cold stares. One young woman, Yolanda, a pregnant 19 years old, stuck her tongue out. Joe fixated on that gesture of unwelcome.

"Joe?" Clarence asked. "Did you hear me?"

"Yes sir." Joe worried aloud, "It probably isn't a good idea to mention to anyone that our old man is the chief, right?"

"Why?"

How could Vince say that, thought Joe. My brother can't be that stupid.

"What?" Clarence wasn't sure what he'd heard.

"Why?" pressed Vince.

Clarence shook his head. He was going to have to school this educated white boy about the world that you don't learn from books.

"The other workers won't take kindly to it. You'll learn soon enough. In the meantime..."

Crash! The impact echoed a wave of sound that woke up the plant. Laughter followed as co-workers reacted hilariously to Elmer running one of the tongues of his forklift into a wall filled with holes.

"Where was I?"

Vince piped up, "In the meantime."

"Oh yeah." Clarence couldn't help but witness a steamy cloud of dust puffing from the just wounded wall. "Stay as far away from Elmer as you can." The dust engulfed the boys. They met Clarence's nod with a nod of their own.

The Richter scale in Dane's head exploded. He forcefully opened a Pullman window and screamed, "Stop running into that wall, dammit!"

Melvyn, the shipping dock supervisor, who felt he should have been named foreman, didn't want Clarence to pay for Elmer's infraction. He yelled back at Dane, "Sir, the fork lift slid on some oil I spilled and failed to clean up. I'm sorry."

Clarence appreciated Melvyn's sense of fair play. Mel could have used the moment to denigrate his former rival, but he resisted the temptation and even protected Elmer.

Dane slammed the window. He hated when he yelled. Yelling was beneath him except when saving life and limb on the links with a vociferous, "Fore."

* * *

Vince and Joe settled in. Their operator Quincy, was a quiet soul who didn't say much. He did as he was told and could care less about who got the summer jobs. He disliked the Beriso boys but kept that to himself. He didn't need any trouble. Like the Beriso's, the job was a ticket to the start of a better life.   Quincy, a young man with bookish thick eyeglasses, had no intention of spending the rest of his life in a factory.

Joe shifted into protect mode. He refused to see who was staring, sticking out their tongue or startled at seeing white skins in jobs that were apparently set to go to black teens.

Quincy stopped the line. He looked up to the catwalk and yelled, "Vat's empty."

Vince and Joe turned to Quincy for direction. He put his hand up and motioned them to sit and take a break.

Frederick and Cedric didn't say much but when they were moved to articulate their thoughts, it could be brutal. "Fred, look at Clarence, giving them panty waists the star treatment."

"Shit," snorted Cedric, "Them white boys will be has-beens when I'm through with 'em."

Frederick gave Cedric a high five followed by a finger shake. "Right on brotha!"   They both smiled like the Devil Incarnate.

"Hey, am I waking you guys up?" Quincy bared his teeth. He didn't like being kept waiting. Operators earned a bonus, based on production. If the line performed well, each crewmember could earn an extra dime an hour also. In this case, Cedric and Frederick were out-of-line, literally and figuratively, standing on the catwalk chewing the fat, making the line wait. What did they care? They didn't reap any of the rewards regarding increased production of a line.

Before Clarence was foreman, he was an operator. He played it smart. He shared his winnings with all of his crew including those on the catwalk. As a result, he didn't net as much as the other operators but he set a standard that few operators emulated, thus making Clarence a man that everyone in the plant valued, respected and in some cases loved. But now he was a foreman and a lot of the luster disappeared upon his ascendency to boss.

For Cedric and Frederick, this was a no-brainer. They were going to tar them white boys till they turned black, only then might they blend in and be welcome. In the minds of these young rebels, that act alone was worthy of the admiration of their co-workers, maybe even a gigantic high-five.

* * *

Clarence sat at a small kitchen table enjoying a cup of steaming coffee as he admired his wife, Jackie. She was beautiful doing anything, even dishes. Clarence loved to take in the nape of Jackie's neck. He loved kidding her about it. He found her sensual.

"So, are you going to talk about it or let it eat at you all night?"

"I'm afraid to tell you," sighed Clarence.

Jackie stopped washing the dish. She dried her hands on a towel next to the sink. She turned. She peered.

"Now, we ain't going to have that. I'm your wife Clarence." She then softened. "You can tell me. I'll still love you."

Clarence shook his head back and forth. He was having a fight with himself. "The guys at the factory let me have it today, when they found out the drawing for those summer jobs went south."

"Can you blame 'em Clarence? You should have been up-front about it when Dane changed the game. Then at least they might be willing to understand."

Clarence squirmed in his seat. "What was I supposed to say? Hey everyone, don't blame me...Dane's the asshole who took away your kids jobs."

Clarence's face dropped into his hands. "I can't put the man on the spot like that. I'd lose my job."

"I still wish you would have given him a piece of your mind."

"No matter what I do, I can't win." Clarence's face sunk into the depths of his hands. He covered his face, his eyes, from the world. "Whether I put my foot down or tell the plant folk the truth, I lose."

Jackie was upset but not with her husband. "Who does Dane think he is? Giving those precious jobs to them two white boys when God knows the kids on the West side need 'em bad."

"Dane's the boss, Jackie. And the boss can do whatever to the little people."

Jackie laughed. "Little people? Oh my, Clarence, I can attest first-hand knowledge that you ain't little people." She glided over to Clarence's lap in a soft swift movement.

The kids were tucked away in their beds. Diedre was sound asleep in her room. When the conditions were right, the ritual of the mating dance took place.

Jackie would do the dishes after she had just served her man a piping cup of coffee. He would bore a hole in the back of her neck and she reciprocated by giving herself to him completely. Ritual was important - especially when it came to sex.

* * *

A radio alarm clock blared with the sound of the *Lovin' Spoonful's, "Summer in the City,"* as the clock flipped from 5:59 to 6:00. Gloria wore a bright yellow housedress that glowed from the morning rays of sun streaming through the windows. "C'mon boys, get up. You'll need extra time for the streetcar. Remember dad's not driving you today, he's on duty and won't be home till later."

Vince and Joe loved their mother dearly. What was there not to love? She was a Cub Scout Den-Mother, a woman deeply invested in her family; a woman with a soft heart that any man or young boy could fall in love with forever. But, even with all that, no woman, in the history of man, has or will ever be appreciated for acting like a rooster. So at those moments they weren't feeling the love. Damn, they had to get up to make the nagging stop. "Shut-up Mom," they screamed in their adolescent male heads. They could never ever say that aloud. Their dad would have killed them for such impudence. That was that.

———

CHAPTER ELEVEN

YOU'RE NOW ONE OF US

At the plant, Melvyn paved cement over the hole in the wall created by Elmer, the wreckful forklift driver. An onerous sounding horn made Melvyn take cover as Elmer flied around a turn and crashed one of the tongues of his forklift into the very hole that had just been paved. Laughter erupted.

One thing about eruptions...they start slowly, but then they expand and sumptuously build and build and build to a sheer maddening climax. Like a finely tuned chorus, laughter, resonated throughout the plant. Even those who couldn't see the act, could hear it...and there was always plenty to laugh about when it came to one of Elmer's crashes. You might not get it till the next day when you heard an eyewitness account, but you laughed just as hard.

Melvyn was pissed. Elmer had damn near gored him to death besides wasting his time to repair the wall...the wall made infamous with Elmer's errant driving. "You bone head!" screamed Melvyn.

Quincy ignored the commotion and set the production line in motion.

Joe and Vince focused on their tasks of sealing and loading fluid canisters of lighter fluid.

"Quincy," asked Vince, "does he do that often?"

Quincy shot Vince a look. He had no intention of becoming buddies with the white boys, but at the same time, he felt compelled to tell them about Elmer, who could wind up killing them. If that happened in a black factory, the city would shut down the plant and then everyone would be screwed. So he answered.

"Often enough."

"Why don't they fire him?"

"Dane feels sorry for Elmer's equilibrium problem."

"His equilibrium problem?" asked Vince.

"Yeah, it means...

"I know what it means," hissed Vince. "I'm surprised you do."

"Really? So, I'm the dumb black guy, right?"

"Well don't make me feel stupid. You started it with 'Yeah, it means,' like, what - I'm stupid?"

"Wow, that's deep. For a split second, I felt a tinge of guilt."

"Fine, I'll take your split second as an apology."

Both men burst out in laughter at such idiocy.

"Damn you white boy, you ought to be on a debate team or something. I'll bet you could make Spam sound good."

"He could," piped in Joe who enjoyed ribbing his brother.

"Dane will never admit it, but, Lucille, his secretary, told me she heard him talking on the phone about Elmer's condition, and she damn near knows everything else about the owner."

Quincy waited to see Vince's reaction.

Vince got the inside joke. Dane was boring.

Both boys realized there was more to Quincy than they expected. In a few short volleys, Vince came to respect Quincy. "So where are you going to college?"

It was a compliment. Quincy compelled himself to return a modicum of respect to the white foreigner. "Loop Junior College. I'll be a sophomore next year."

"Yeah, me too. So, what's your goal?"

"To be a doctor. But for now, I need to help my Mom. I go to school at night, so it takes a bit longer. I've been going for three years. I'm just starting my sophomore year of college."

"That's a tough schedule."

"If you want it bad enough...you do what must be done."

A yellow warning strobe light started to spin. "Shit this vat's empty." Quincy locked the vat gate's safety valve. Quincy leaned his head out to peruse the catwalk. He was looking for Fred or Cedric. "Vat's empty," yelled Quincy to the world above.

Fred and Cedric eyed each other. Cedric pushed the empty vat onto a roller track into position for a refill. Fluids came to the plant via huge tanker trucks. Each liquid had its own connection pipe. So each of the six fluids dispensed at Anderson came from unique storage containers that could be routed to any vat and any production line. Any line could be adapted to fit any sized canister. Using a unique locking system, the vat had to travel about three feet from the feeder railroad of roller wheel gauge. As the vat traveled over Vince and Joe towards its locking position, the vat unexpectedly burst, drenching the white boys in petroleum.

Cedric said it loud enough for others nearby to hear. "Now, you're one of us."

Vince and Joe struggled with the slimy mess.

"You did that on purpose!" Vince's eyes burned red like the brake lights on a car.

"I don't know what you talkin' about white boy."

An alarm sounded. Red lights flashed. Dane arose from the dead in his office squinting from a nap interrupted. He searched for the problem but his focus was on the wrong side of the plant.

Clarence shook his head at the sight of the boys trailing oil that shined like blood as sunshine bounced off the spill on the floor. "You two need to clean up."

The boys headed quickly into the locker room.

"I saw what you did Fred."

"What you talkin' about? It was an accident."

"Accident my ass. Now besides gettin' those white boys full of oil, you've just shut down a line for at least half-an-hour. Now my ass is on the line. Clean up this mess and do it quickly or your ass is going to be out-the-door."

"Hell no. That's what the wetback's for. Get Diego." Fred didn't care what Clarence thought.

"Why we gots to do it?" demanded Cedric. "You siding with those white boys?"

Clarence had enough.

"You two want to discuss it? Cause if you do, let's go upstairs now and get Dane involved. You sure you want that?"

Fred shook his head no to Cedric. He didn't have to. They knew they'd be better off with Clarence, even if he was a Tom at times, than that crazy ass Danish upstairs.

Fred and Cedric in plain sight of Clarence, looked at each other. Their conspiracy was complete. Clarence jumped on it.

"And don't you think that I believe for one moment you're clean in this Cedric. Cause you ain't! You know it and so do I. You get your hands dirty too! I want it cleaned up now!"

* * *

The overalls protected their clothes from most of the oily residue but they smelled awful and their hair sparkled with a lacquered look.

Their fellow passengers on CTA Route 37 stared at the boys wondering singularly and collectively, "What the hell happened to them?" Chicago Transit Authority riders and drivers had seen it all, but this was worth noting and paying attention to.

Joe didn't like the looks. "I'm not going back tomorrow."

"You telling dad that?" Vince stared at his brother. "Are you Joe?"

"Look at us Vince, We look like buffoons."

Vince was insistent, "We're not backing down."

"Why not?"

Vince fumed. "Because a Beriso doesn't back down."

* * *

John, with reading glasses on, skimmed UNDERSTANDING GREEK MYTHOLOGY as he reclined in his Lazy Boy chair. His concentration was broken when Vince and Joe appeared. "What the hell happened to you two?"

John's boisterous inquiry drew Gloria from the kitchen. Her initial shock turned to anger. "Oh, my God! Those animals did this to you, didn't they?"

Vince hesitated. Joe jumped in. "There was an accident on the line."

"Mom, it's nothing," pleaded Vince.

Gloria's wrath turned squarely at John. "They're in good hands, huh?"

"What?" John hated when his wife beat up on him, even when she was right.

"Boys, I'm returning to the kitchen and you are going to hit the shower. Dinner will be ready in about twenty minutes, don't be late!"

As the boys slowly moved up the stairs, John let them have it. "You two better learn to stand up for yourselves. I didn't raise no wussies."

After uttering those words, John found Gloria nose-to-nose in his face. "No need to get worked up, Gloria. I'll handle it."

"You better, John!" Gloria returned to the kitchen.

John sheepishly joined her. Gloria knew she had won and yet she didn't feel good about it. She loved her husband for trying to help the boys get summer jobs but for her man to think he could control something so out of control such as racial relations - was sheer stupidity or sheer arrogance. Either way it didn't matter. In Gloria's mind, her sons had been dropped smack dab in the heart of a combat zone as deadly as Vietnam.

* * *

Clarence answered a ringing phone in the etiquette of 1968 America, "Wilson residence."

From a suburban location, where lavish homes with outdoor swimming pools were the norm, stretched Dane, adorned in a spa robe on a Barcalounger, holding a cigarette in one hand, a drink in the other and a phone cradled in his ear. His two kids were at his feet splashing in the pool while his trophy wife, wearing a striking itsy-bitsy polka-dot bikini, served him a fresh drink. "Clarence, the Chief called me tonight. I was amazed that he could even get my home number but when someone in government, even a fire chief, wants to find you, they can." Dane waited for Clarence to say something.

Clarence flattened his back into the wall. What the hell could he say that would make sense? Best to keep quiet.

"Clarence, why the hell didn't you tell me about the boys being doused with oil?" Dane waited for an answer. All he got was an...

"Uh."

"Clarence, that's not an answer. Can you tell me why I had to hear shit from this pain-in-the-ass fireman tonight, without being forewarned? You know I hate surprises!"

This time Clarence refused to utter an "uh."

"Yeah, you'd better be quiet," hissed Dane. "There's no excuse for that. None."

Clarence winced, but still no "uh."

"You've got one strike buddy. Now I suggest you start taking control of that floor, if, you want to remain my foreman."

Clarence responded immediately. "Yes sir."

"Good! Finally we get more than a grunt out of you."

Even the bikini clad trophy wife found that one funny as she flashed a dazzling set of whites followed with a naughty toss of her head.

"So let's make sure we don't have a failure to communicate. I don't want another call from that guy regarding those boys. Got it?"

"Yes, sir. Won't happen again."

A matronly black woman, with the look of an Aunt Jemima, came to escort the kids off to the house and tuck them off to bed. She, like Aunt Jemima, was the smiling, good Negro, that everyone could trust, maybe even love. Besides all that, Dane loved her yummy pancakes.

Dane took a deep puff on his cigarette and jingled the ice in his drink as he imbibed, loud enough for Clarence to hear through the phone.

"Goooood! See you tomorrow."

Clarence hung up the phone exhausted. He seethed but not at Dane. Dane was doing his job. He was being frank. He made his point, directly, the way a man should treat another man in business. Dane may have been a bit of a racist, but not in business. In business all men were equal. That search for the almighty dollar was something any man could respect another man about, no matter what the color. That was a creed Dane was raised by. Except for the sarcastic, "Goooood," Clarence felt Dane had been fair in his criticism.

If there was anybody Clarence had a right to be upset with, it was Cedric and Fred, who were jeopardizing the peace. Cedric and Fred had drawn a line in the sand. They may have won this battle but only because Clarence let them. Clarence drifted from reason to irritable emotion - damn those white boys and damn their racist father.

———

CHAPTER TWELVE

I CRUSH YOUR HEAD

At dinner in the Beriso home, Vince looked down in disappointment. Joe rose to the occasion and tried to protect his brother by proclaiming that Vince's conviction to stay the course had won the day.

Joe, just as he had when they were little kids, ages 4 and 5 was fierce in his loyalty to his brother. As the story went, John witnessed from a window Vince being bullied by what he estimated was an eight or nine year old kid. John knew how to teach his oldest son a lesson and at the same time tap into the mind of his youngest, which had no fear and no shame. John handed his son a baseball bat. John opened the shade so that Joe could see a big kid pestering his sibling.

"Joey, I want you to take this bat and tell that big kid, bothering Vince, 'you touch my brother, I'll knock your head off.'"

The way the story's always been told, Joe scared the shit out of the big kid, as he murderously swished the airspace near his noggin, chanting, "I want to knock your block off."

But Gloria had a way of shattering that dynamic set by John and the boys when they tried to convince the woman of the house that all was just fine.

"My God, John! Those animals at that factory did something horrible to my babies. It shouldn't have happened. Why did it?"

Every testicle in the room winced on "babies." Gloria didn't suffer fools gladly. She allowed the men to think at times that she was a step behind when in fact she was always a step ahead. She knew exactly what she was doing with the word, "babies." She wanted to piss off each and every testicle.

"Aw Mom, it's nothing."

"Nothing Vince?"

Gloria locked her eyes on her husband's. "They're in good hands, huh?"

John shrugged. He didn't know what to say. If he said anything, the boys or worse his wife could use it against him. Sometimes silence was golden.

"John, my confidence in you has waned."

"Geezes Gloria. Waned? What's that...is that a real word or are you screwing with me?"

"Waned is a real word. I'm disappointed in your inability to protect our boys."

"Wow, that hurts."

John dropped his eyes. Gloria had every right to voice an opinion, but so often she'd refrain from exercising that option. She believed that a woman should follow her man. She was old fashioned in that way. But it made her feel so much more in the bedroom when her man made passionate love to her...saying the things every woman no matter how young or how old wants to hear, "you're gorgeous, you're beautiful and I'm passionate about you," made the role playing worth it. She knew he really loved his woman. And yet on rare occasions she asked him to put his opinion aside and follow her advice. She did not want "her babies" to go to work on hot summer days in the aftermath of a war zone. The race riots in April left scars, huge scars over the landscape of America's cities.

John waited as long as he could. "What do you want me to say?"

"Promise me this," she looked at her sons, showered but still looking oily, "it doesn't happen again."

* * *

Clarence somehow got the phone on the hook as he slid down the wall. The pain in his gut burned soulfully. It had only taken Dane 90 seconds to destroy Clarence's self-esteem. He buried his head in his hands. He whacked his head from both sides. "Those damn white boys."

* * *

Melvyn and Reggie unloaded boxes from the back of a semi-truck and stacked them on a pallet. The pallet was almost full.

"Get a move on man! I don't want to be all day at this."

"Ain't me Melvyn. Elmer's moving like old people fuck."

"Quit your hacking Reg. I'm doing my fair share and I was up all night making Sheila squeal."

Reggie smiled. "Sheila? You went a round with that sweat hog. Man, how many beers did you have at the club last night?"

"It don't feel bad in the dark and she gives good head."

"Really?"

Both men busted with laughter.

"Although you do have to watch out for the dark sometimes. Man I got tagged so bad once that when I took home this foxy lady, it turned out her's was bigger than mine."

Reggie's eyes widened with curiosity.

"So what'd you do Melvyn?"

"I'm not one to kiss and tell."

Reggie looked shocked.

Melvyn smiled a look of, "gothcha!"

Reggie reacted to Melvyn's joke. "Oh, shit you had me man."

"I kicked his ass to the curb," pronounced Melvyn proudly.

Reggie acknowledged the obvious with a nod until he heard Melvyn state, "but only after he gave me a blow job."

Reggie took the bait, looking shocked until Melvyn winked at him. Both men cracked smiles followed by hearty laughter.

Elmer's forklift turned the corner.

"Even Elmer wouldn't stoop that low," Reggie insisted.

"Elmer wouldn't know where to find it," spat Melvyn as a coffee looking hack-of-tobacco bounced off the interior curve of a coffee colored trashcan.

Elmer lined up the forklift tongs under the palette. He noticed Reggie and Melvyn laughing.

Melvyn fought back his laughter as he asked the question. "Ever spread a butterfly?"

Elmer giggled. "Y'all taw…tawk…tawkin' SEX? Ain't ya."

Like TV anchors on a news show, they split the read. "Yeah Elmer."

"You ought to try it sometime."

Elmer lifted the loaded pallet, reversed, turned away from the dock and stopped. He looked back at Melvyn and Reggie. "Aw, ya know, I done told ya, a..ah..ah hunnerd times." He pulled away from the conversation of coitus, screaming above the din as he gunned his forklift and became a blur. "Remember. Mar..Mar...Mariage first... then sex!"

On the other side of the plant, Clarence sequestered Vince and Joe to what he hoped would be safe if not friendly confines. Faye operated the lighter-fluid production line. Clarence prayed that they'd be safe there. "Today, you boys'll be working the end of Faye's belt."

Clarence looked at Faye to acknowledge if not welcome the boys to her line. She ignored them.

"And this here is Sandra." Clarence pointed to the small but very pregnant Sandra at the top of the line. "She loads the canisters onto the belt that moves onto Faye, who dispenses the fluids."

Sandra continued to work and with little effort reprimanded the boys she had just met. "You two, stay over there away from me and we be fine."

The boys looked to Clarence for guidance. None was forthcoming except a call to trust.

"You'll be in good hands. My word."

Clarence exited. Faye shot him a look of deadpan disgust. She then fired up the line for a day of production. A day in which Sandra, stationed at the front of the line, would set the pace. Faye, at the heart of the line, operated the controls like a captain standing on a bridge guiding the craft into port. The boys served as the backbone of the line; lifting, leveraging, loading boxes laden with liquids that ranged from the deep cabaret color of petroleum to the fire engine red of transmission oil.

As the day wore on, the four team members settled in. The boys were strong. They could carton quickly, meaning production moved faster. That meant more money for everyone, and if ever there was an equalizer in life, the ability to put more dollars in one's pocket made it near impossible to hate a hard worker. Money for black or white was hard to find in 1968 due in part to the war, the assassinations, the riots, the racial divide wreaking havoc on the worker. If those boys provided a way to make more money, Faye and Sandra could care less about their whiteness. But that all flowed only if the boys didn't ask stupid questions like, "We can wear slippers here?"

"Sho can, if you'se pregnant." Sandra didn't appreciate the question. "Who was Mr. Vince to question me?" she thought but somehow could not come to say it.

"What's that got to do with being pregnant?"

Now it was Faye's turn and she planned to ream him. "Don't cha know anything about women? Ask your Mama if her feet hurt when you big lugs were in her oven."

"Well of course I know about women," contended Vince. "I am after all, pre-med. What Sandra should be doing is resting at home."

"Resting?" challenged Sandra.

"Mothafffffff" wheezed Faye as she stressed her "f's."

Money or no money, Sandra couldn't stand it. She was screaming inside. "Maybe in your 'Leave It To Beaver' world, but in my house I'm the breadwinner."

Now Joe took his turn being a naive asshole. "Where's your husband?"

Sandra bit down on her tongue. "Ain't got one. Don't need one. Doin' fine without one."

Vince felt slighted, then offended. "Yeah, we've heard that's common."

Faye smiled for the first time that day. "Yeah, that don't speak well for you men folk, do it?"

What could they say? Faye had trumped their insult with one that was squarely aimed at the inherent failure of men, whether they were black, yellow, red or white.

* * *

"Hey, get your shit out of here." Clarence hated when "Hot Man" showed up in front of the factory pushing a loaded shopping cart filled with an array of merchandise. Everybody knew the stuff was hot. The only ones not on to "Hot Man" were the "POH-LEASE." They never gave the "nigga" any respect. I mean why would you? "He's a nigger and a bum too. How low is that?" queried every one of Chicago's finest who rumbled past him on the street in their squad.

"Aw Clarence, I'm just trying to survive. C'mon, what's wrong with you?"

"Nothing. You think the cops don't know you're trading hot shit? Hot Shit-Man."

"Hey now, none of that...it's Hot Man...every body knows that."

For Clarence, "Hot Man" was the epitome of disdain - the shiftless, lazy cartoon character adorned in black face singing, "My sweet mammie, how I love you, how I love you." It was visceral. "Take it somewhere else or I'm calling the cops."

"You do that. I'd probably have better luck with them."

When "Hot Man" ignored Clarence, the foreman used a look that said to those that gave "Hot Man" the time of day, "If you value your jobs, you'll have none of it."

"What's your problem brother?" "Hot Man" confronted Clarence.

"Your price is too high."

"What d'ya mean? I got some of the meanest prices."

"Your price supports the myth that blacks do nothing but steal. Ever consider that?"

"Where else can I go on this block? I sure ain't about to cross that viaduct. Them white boys will surely make me pay." The fear "Hot Man" felt was primal.

"I don't care," screamed Clarence. "When your stuff's not hot, you'll be welcome. Until then, it's no way, nada, nyet! Nein, Nein, Nein! How many ways can I say no?"

* * *

A 1968 champagne gold Chevy Impala sedan rolled into the Beriso driveway. John honked the horn as the radio blasted Dinah Shore's, "See The U.S.A. In A Chevrolet." For those not in the know to this reference, golden southern girl Dinah Shore, wowed the television audience in the early 1950's with a variety show that America watched and more importantly enjoyed. Dinah was a hit and one of the things that may have made her so enduring with the public was her rendition of "See The U.S.A. In A Chevrolet." It was a live jingle-like commercial. But it was also the exit of Dinah's show. People were mesmerized by her rendition of that song. It was an experience that can't be realized except in that particular moment of time.

John let the car run as he sat back and admired the interior dash. He yelled out the car window. "Gloria, boys, get out here!"

Gloria and Vince responded quickly, with Joe a bit in the rear. "Why the commotion? Oh my God! John, did you buy a new car?"

"Cool looking wheels, Dad!" Vince was in a squat checking out a wheel cover.

Joe, the last to arrive wondered out loud, "Whose wheels are they?"

"They're mine...I mean ours." John recovered quickly when he made an obvious faux pas. It didn't mean that the others didn't feel a barb or two, but that's just what they'd all came to expect from the man, their husband, father and fearless leader.

"And we can afford this?" could only come from the one person who had free reign to question the Battalion Chief.

"With that fire inspecting job I just got, yeah."

The boys loved to watch their mother squeeze their father. They loved their dad. He was solidly in their corner. But if they loved their father, they worshipped their mother. They feared their father so every now and then it was a treat to watch the old man sweat.

Whenever they saw their father at work, they witnessed a commander, a demi-god, who everyone had to pay homage to. The only one that could engender fear into their father's eyes was their mother. Their parents enjoyed a relationship where the man (John) wore the pants in the house but his woman (Gloria) controlled who slept in their bed, and that's real power. John hated sleeping on the couch, he knew there would be more questions.

"Did you get a deal on the trade-in?"

"No, I kept it for the boys."

That created a smile on Gloria's face. Her man had done right by her kids. She loved her kids and whoever loved them she loved even more. John knew that about Gloria. That's why he didn't trade in the car. Giving it to the boys would make Gloria happy. There are days in a man's life when he wants to celebrate. That day is not complete until a man ravages the woman he loves. Passion was something every man craved on days when he won a battle in life. John, pleased that the new job provided a car at dealer cost - all part of an elaborate trade deal Mercury Insurance worked out with a local dealership - gave the Beriso patriarch hope that better days were ahead. How many men get the opportunity to buy a dealer car with less than 3,000 miles on it; practically a new car below cost? Unless you told them, nobody would suspect the car as anything but brand new. In the '60's that was crucial. Keeping up with the neighbors was the weave in the fabric of life at the time.

"Wow, we're getting the convertible!" Vince stood up from his squat.

"Yeah, tune it up and you're set," smiled John upon his sons.

"No more having to ride the bus." Joe blurted bubbling over.

"Ahhhh, no."

Both boys just stared at their father's answer as it hung out to dry. They couldn't believe it and together asked, "Why?"

John hesitated. Gloria spotted the weakness and hit pay dirt with, "What do you mean, 'no?'"

John looked at the boys. He refused to give Gloria any satisfaction. There was a line in the sand that she damn well better not cross, ever. His refusal to make intimate eye contact with the Love of his life was his way of saying it without saying it, "Don't embarrass or second guess me in front of *my* boys." It was "our" boys when Love came in peace.

"Around here and to school, that's okay, but that baby's in mint condition and it ain't going down in that neighborhood."

"Hmm, 'mint condition' is it?" The "it" had ever so slightly a lilt of sarcasm that John got "it" even if the boys didn't. "Well then I guess the car deserves all the protection it can get but shouldn't your own flesh and blood deserve at least the same?" That sarcasm was apparent to all.

"So you're still steaming about them working in my district?"

John shook his head in disbelief. Gloria broke the one and only rule that John ever put in place. She was lucky. Most wives, of that time, were burdened with scores of rules. Men were thought to be controlling by the opposite sex.

"C'mon guys, we're taking a ride. I left your car back at the dealer's."

Gloria wouldn't accept the dismissal. "Well since you're going to be out, stay out for a while." Gloria was disappointed. Her boys had sold themselves out. They had acquiesced to their father, when she needed their support most. The allure of having a car, even if it only could be driven on the "right" side of the city of Chicago was too much for them to pass up.

John, pissed that the protest continued, refused to show his anger. In a sweet voice came the words, "And just what would you recommend we do that would be long enough for you?"

Gloria stepped up and into the face of her man. The boys could hear some of what she said. "I don't care what you do, but you'd better do something for them boys. They're both interested in golf even if you're not. Maybe they can show you their swing; that would mean a great deal to them. You might even consider hitting one." Gloria began to walk backwards towards her home. It was "her home" when he was being an asshole.

But the next outburst was targeted to strike all. She was hurt that her husband refused to please her and disappointed that her boys (they were "her" boys when he controlled them) had not held with their mother. That really hurt. And yet it seemed contradictory, even to her. If life were a giant cartoon, Gloria's thought bubble read, "I blame him for trying to control them and yet that's exactly what he's got me doing." But back to the matter at hand, the boys' eyes averted those of their mother. They squirmed like traitors, but hey, it was a car. A car was freedom, sex and rock and roll.

Gloria got it, but that hardly stopped her from sharing her disgust with her men. "Don't worry; I'm sure they'll bow low enough to put your big ball on a tee."

CHAPTER THIRTEEN

R-E-S-P-E-C-T

While Joe and Vince sat comfortably in their home with mom and dad watching TV, Quincy, the operator of the line shuffled down a dark street with a backpack loaded with books. P-STONE gang members, seated on a rusted car on a burned out lot, watched.

"Hey school boy!" shouted the leader of the group.

Quincy was smart enough to know that he had to pay the man respect if he was going to get home that night. "I know, I know, when am I ever gonna realize, I mean learn, that books are fo'suckers...right?"

The leader smiled. "That's right...when?"

"When my grandmother dies. Ya'know, she's really sick and she wants me to go to school and...well, I'm only doing it for her." Quincy always took a beat to see how the leader would react. Only then did Quincy volunteer, "You can dig that, right?"

It was always gibberish about his grandmother, his mother and his little sister. Even P-Stone rangers like their grandmothers, mothers and sisters. He'd just kill with that stuff and would then be allowed to continue his journey home. On the way he witnessed the visual of Senator Robert...Bobby Kennedy on TV screens in the windows of the appliance stores on Stony Island Avenue.

In the Beriso living room, the voice and visage of RFK could be clearly heard and witnessed live on TV. "I would hope now that the California primary is finished, now that the primary is over, and that we can now concentrate on having a dialogue...on what direction we want to go in the United States: What we're going to do in the rural areas of this country; What we're going to do for those who still suffer in the United States from hunger; What we're going to do around the rest of the globe; and whether we're going to continue the policies which have been so unsuccessful in Vietnam. I think we should move in a different direction...so my thanks to all of you. And now it's on to Chicago and let's win there!"

The crowd cheered Bobby and though Quincy couldn't hear the affirmation through the glass showcase windows, he could feel the euphoria of the crowd as TV images captured the excitement of that moment.

Flashing cameras, spotlights and cheering supporters were suddenly quieted with the sound of gunfire. It really didn't matter whether you sat in the comfortable living room with sound or braved the night on Stony Island Avenue and felt the rumble of sound against glass dissipate to nothing.

"Must America murder all of their visionaries?" That was the question asked by people of every shade of white, black, yellow or red. Many of those shades seethed with anger and coveted revenge even if they stopped short of actually seeking it.

And when no answer was forthcoming the different shades asked, "Why Lord, why another one?"

At that moment, the hopes and dreams of many lost faith, heart and charity.

* * *

Thursday morning June 6, 1968 newspapers showcased a higher than usual headline alerting the world that it was Robert F. Kennedy less. In just five years, two brothers paid the ultimate price of assassination. No matter what your politics, at that time in America, the majority of people grieved over the loss...and those who didn't had the good sense to keep it to themselves. It's called civility and how good would it be to have it back?

So it's no surprise that when Joe and Vince offered Reggie and Larry a warm "Good morning," it was met with hostility.

"What's so damn good about it? Haven't you read the paper, don't you know what happened?"

"Oh yeah, that's a shame." Vince's weak answer fired up Larry.

"A shame. Shiiiiit, it's a wee bit more than a shame if you're a black man." Larry shook his head in disbelief of what he saw as stupidity or insincerity. Either way, Vince's stock dropped with Reggie.

"Ok, so we don't know. So teach us." Joe said what Vince wanted to but couldn't.

Reggie's stock of Joe skyrocketed. "How's you two white boys, almost men, don't know? I don't know why you wouldn't know unless you're sheltered."

Reggie saw their look. It was clear, they lived a life far from the real world. This moment could be pivotal, an eye-opening experience for two white boy who didn't have a clue on why a black man would weep at the loss of a Bobby Kennedy in a way, a white man would never, could never truly understand. Reggie's irritation itched but he needed patience...the patience of a mentor, a teacher, a rabbi, a minister, and a priest. Reggie sensed that this split second of his life meant a lot to the boys, to himself and to bridging the great divide between what's black and what's white. "Bobby and John Kennedy offered us hope. They seemed to give-a-shit about the colored man. Maybe they were great actors, but if they was, they sure had us fooled." Reggie's voice cracked emotion, "We believed and trusted a Kennedy as president and begged God for a better life. It ain't no fun being a Nigger."

Melvyn had pulled his forklift alongside the mini-meeting. He was flush with the need to say something. "He was our great white hope." Maybe if the boys knew, truly understood, the importance of what happened they could understand why the people at the plant felt awful, bitter, hostile and downright sick at the site of the morning headlines, "RFK Assassinated."

"What about LBJ?" Joe asked for himself and his curious brother. "After all it was LBJ who kick-started the civil rights legislation that Kennedy tried to get through Congress but couldn't." Everyone knew that LBJ would get it done. He was a master politician who could wrangle the votes necessary to push the bill through. John Kennedy was a Clydesdale, LBJ was a workhorse...but an amazing one that could actually deliver the goods.

"LBJ don't care if colored folk are canon fodder." Melvyn joined the conversation and looked for accolade, the gentle touch of a sword on his shoulder bestowing a knighthood-of-respect that often his colleagues failed to recognize.

"Got that right!" Larry yelled. At once, Melvyn felt good, like he belonged.

Larry was disgusted by the events of the night before. "Like you've heard, Bobby was our great white hope. But you can forget that, now that he's gone."

"Yeah," Melvyn, confident that he earned his knighthood, ventured, " Bobby wanted to end Vietnam."

Fred and Cedric joined the conclave...a gathering that had caught the eye of Clarence. Fred ripped. "All I know is finally a white boy, a rich one at that, got one in the head."

"What you go and say somethin' stupid like that," Larry fumed.

"That's wrong. Dead wrong." Reggie deadpanned but refused to engage in the laughter that the two troublemakers enjoyed with his timely use of the word dead.

"You can say that again, old man...you're funny." Cedric finally found his voice.

"Nothing funny about it. Bobby Kennedy was more than some white rich boy...he was the best we got after they killed Martin." Reggie relived a moment of complete and utter sorrow, the kind that pangs in your gut and stings at your heart. Martin Luther King was this/close to God in Reggie's heart. He missed him. He had met Martin Luther King Jr. once, when the citizens that lived in the Marquette Park neighborhood decided to stone the reverend. Chicago was and will always be a city of neighborhoods, often identified by the local park. Vince and Joe understood that. They hailed from the Portage Park neighborhood, named after the major park in their community.

Cedric listened. He sensed Reggie's pain but he was not going to let anyone rip on Fred. "Fred ain't off. We done had our turn with Martin. But it don't matter, cuz anyone for darkie is getting one in the head."

"Well, no one should get shot over trying to help people." Reggie, Cedric, Fred and Melvyn couldn't believe they heard those words of wisdom from white-boy-Joe who didn't know that silence at times could be golden.

Finally Cedric broke the silence. "Who asked you white-boy?"

"You can't argue with that, Cedric." Reggie's answer seemed apparent, but somewhat cryptic. "Should one get shot for trying to make the world a better place?"

Clarence grabbed his P.A. microphone, "Hey it's time to get a move on. Let's go to work." He kept his eyes glued on the conclave till it busted up. Melvyn zipped away on his forklift as Fred and Cedric climbed to the catwalk of the vats above the production lines. Clarence dropped a needle on a Tony Williams record rolling on a turntable hooked into the P.A. The music awakened the plant as the roar of production lines firing up punctuated the beat of jazz laid down by Tony. Reggie walked with the boys to their lines.

"Man those guys are racists." Vince was amazed that he had said it rather than leave the difficult task of speaking brazenly to his younger brother.

"Say what?" Reggie was flabbergasted. In his mind he could literally hear the words, "Had a white-boy just called a black man - a racist? That can't be."

"They really hate us white people, don't they?" Joe's inquisition was a hard right turn from foolishness to fear.

"Look, Fred and Cedric have been through enough in their lifetime to feel threatened by white people. What you see as animosity is nothing more than them having their guard up. It ain't all black and white," Reggie continued.

"Seems that way to me." Vince wasn't in the mood to be apologetic.

"Then you don't know the difference between being a racist and being prejudiced." Reggie was losing his patience just as they broke up to go different ways. The boys talked as they walked to their line.

"Where'd that guy get off telling us the difference between those two words?" Vince didn't appreciate Reggie's admonishment.

Joe stopped and listened to the music. He recognized the tune. "I'll catch up with you in a minute." Joe walked toward the source of the music.

"Well, hurry up cuz I don't wanna be stuck alone with those two wackos." Vince cocked his head back at the women on his line, the bitter Faye and the beleaguered Sandra.

Joe nodded, turned and interrupted Clarence busy in paperwork. *"This Here*, by Tony Williams...right?"

"So you like Tony?" Now Clarence was intrigued. "You play?"

"Yeah. I got a boss set of Gretsch tom-toms with a Rogers' snare and pedal. The bass drum is a 24 inch...it kicks ass." Joe loved to talk drum gear.

"Sweet set-up. That's Tony's set-up, ain't it?"

Joe smiled, "He's my favorite drummer."

"I saw Tony play at Mr. Kelly's last year. He was somethin' else." The bond he felt for this kid surprised Clarence. Music, oh sweet music can do that to people...it can bring them together in a way that unites the soul in all of us.

"Wow I wish I could see him, but my father would never let me do that."

"Your dad's um...strict, isn't he?"

"That's being diplomatic Clarence. The fact is he doesn't want to see me live my life in nightclubs."

Clarence extended a slight nod. He didn't know what else to do and then it came to him as if a spirit took control of his mouth and out came the words, "Tell you what."

Clarence pulled the record off its turntable, sliding it into the album cover. The cacophonous cough of machinery sputtered as flasks filled full of fluid crackled with a distinct footprint of sound dependent on what the cannisters were made of, tin or aluminum. For many, the music was background but for Clarence and those who felt the beat the way he did, it was nirvana. The music broke the monotony, the grind of factory work.

"Until you get to see Tony, be my guest." Clarence handed the LP to Joe.

Joe looked at the record in astonishment. "Oh, I can't take this."

"Sure you can, I've got a copy at home." A beam of sun crashed through a window overhead onto the two men. Clarence's gesture shocked Joe. In a new light, Joe saw a man that he really liked. "Cool, thanks man!"

"I'd sure like to see you play sometime."

Joe hesitated for a nano-second, but still long enough to be felt.

"Yeah, maybe someday."

Wes, one of the oldest workers in the plant had been standing patiently to talk with Clarence. He heard the exchange between Joe and Clarence. As soon as Joe was out of range, Wes laughed into Clarence's face, making the foreman ill at ease. "You know Clarence, that 'maybe someday' ain't going to happen in one lifetime and I doubt it'll come to pass in two."

CHAPTER FOURTEEN

UP CLOSE & PERSONAL

Faye stirred a large pot of red beans and rice. The smell of a slight tinge of curry gave the concoction a sweetness that made the dish savory. It was her son Lawrence's favorite dish and thank God. Red beans and rice was a cheap, carb-loaded, calorie leavened meal that stuck to you.

The creak on the back-porch steps brought relief to Faye's face. The door opened. Lawrence appeared, disappointed.

"Why you so late son?"

"Mama, I promised myself I wouldn't come home without a job...but here I am with nothing but frustration."

"Oh you gots to keep the faith, baby. You'll find something." Faye steamed each time she heard herself say those words. The steam would be followed by a visage, the appearance of Clarence in her mind.

"And what if I don't find 'something' Mama, What then?"

Faye could feel the pain in the warble of her son's voice. He was done, overdone and fearful of experiencing life up close and personal in a Vietcong jungle.

"Let's not think negative Lawrence. The Lord says, 'be of good courage' so that's what we must do. Now go wash up. This gumbo will be ready any minute."

Lawrence moped rather than smile at his mom. He was pissed that she failed to deliver on her promise to secure him a summer job with Anderson, Inc. Lawrence damn well believed he deserved it. He worked tirelessly to be the valedictorian of his class. He had come through, why couldn't adults hold up their end?

Faye could feel her son's frustration and his utter disappointment "If my mother says it, then you can count on it being gospel," was a phrase he often invoked in the name of his Mama. The thought made Faye cringe with anger. "Damn that Clarence and damn them white boys. How dare he give them a place when he knows how hard my boy worked."

Faye hurt inside. She slammed the spoon on the stovetop. She cried. "God, please protect and save my boy!"

Faye looked to a window filled with the backyard. There it was. It was the swing; filled with her baby Lawrence. That's the image she remembered. *The promise of new life swings in the balance on a grand, great black oak tree.*

* * *

John stood bent in front of the television, cranking the channel changer. Gloria sat on the sofa. She liked to knit. On the television a black reporter addressed the camera and began his report with a question, "How is the tragic death of Bobby Kennedy going to affect black voters come this November?"

John cranked the channel. "Who cares?"

The next visual to appear on screen was Martin Luther King delivering his iconic "I Have A Dream" speech accompanied by John's sigh. "Geeze Louise, nothing but niggers!" John paused long enough to let Martin share part of his dream.

"Where little black boys and black girls will be able to join hands with little white boys and white girls and walk together as sisters and brothers. I have a dream today --

John looked. He shook his head "No way nigger." He cranked the channel again. "Keep dreaming. Not in our lifetimes." The hiss of empty channels echoed until the crank lead to a screen filled with Nat King Cole crooning "Mona Lisa, Mona Lisa."

"Hey Gloria, this looks good." Gloria looked over her knitting. She stopped what she was doing and smiled back at John, pleased that he had found something worth watching. It didn't matter that Nat King Cole was the same color as Martin, Nat was entertaining and mild mannered.

"I remember this episode," convinced that she had seen it. She liked to tease John.

"Nah, we haven't seen him do Mona Lisa. It looks like it's from one of his live shows."

Gloria would shoot John a play-it-dumb look. She loved to make her man feel smart. She had the nursing degree and had gone to college; he missed high school. As soon as he graduated from grammar school, he was made to go to work, for the sake of the family. Family was everything. He had sacrificed a lot. He liked learning. Maybe that was why he made Battalion Chief. He would prove them wrong. He would prove himself right. He went far because he never quit reading. Reading made one smarter.

"John, how can you tell the difference between whether it's film or a recording from a live show?"

"TV cameras have a harsh look about them. Film reminds me more of charcoal paintings. It's got a warmer look."

"Charcoal paintings? How so?"

This was a moment, as a couple, to share in whatever new thing John had discovered. That seemed to some in her family circle of friends, like a lop-sided relationship. She didn't care. Gloria was proud of him; proud of how he struggled to attain rank. She knew better than anyone, being a "Coleen" herself, that it was tough for an Italian to crack the Irish dominance of anything and everything in the city of Chicago. But here he was, the first and only Italian Battalion Chief on the force in 1968.

"C'mon you know I've been to the TV stations. You can see it in the light." John pointed to a portion of the screen. He then switched the channel that had a movie running. You could see the difference. The light in the background looked soft and even softer in the foreground of the shot. As he switched back to Nat King Cole, Gloria saw the difference. Everything live on TV looked harsher. An observation she had failed to notice but one that her man helped her to see.

She knelt next to her husband in front of the TV as he squat to adjust the sound. "So which one am I?" Gloria looked deep into John's eyes. "C'mon which light would I be on a TV or movie set?"

John shifted. He now was on one knee. He took her head in his hands. He kissed her. "You're always a movie set. The light in the background is soft but you're the softest." He kissed her over and over whispering what she loved to hear "...you're my light, my shining light."

* * *

A banner that stretched from one side of the street to the other, read: "THE 8TH ANNUAL BAPTIST CHURCH 4TH of JULY BLOCK PARTY."

The Hope Baptist block party was probably the only time when all of the parishioners came together. The Reverend Clemmons flock was ten thousand strong. He gave three services each Sunday, one at eight, one at 10 and one at Noon. Clemmons had an assistant, but he was tolerated only during the two weeks when the Reverend took a vacation or if he was sick, which was rare.

Dancers sashayed to the music of Duke Ellington's "Satin Doll," cooks flipped sizzling barbecue and friends toasted one another with a nip, sip or two. Sista O'Dell sat at a table. She was passionate, consumed might be more accurate, with the need to register new voters. Change was not going to come until the Negro realized the power of the ballot.

Jackie and Clarence found the block party an opportune time to celebrate their romance. The kids disappeared with a pack of friends armed with sparklers. Diedre followed suit by seeking out old friends and catching up on time gone by. On this night they were left alone to be a couple again.

A couple that found each other interesting. God made a man and from man woman was made; the woman took the devil's apple and the devil gave their relationship a spark that they craved...physically, emotionally and spiritually. When God first made man, he gave him paradise, and when paradise was forever lost, it was that devil in a woman that made a man feel like he was in paradise again.

They danced and danced amongst a cornucopia of characters: the Shaman looking bum stomping his foot on the ground as he wailed on his harmonica; a "Water Melon Man" moving like Jackity-Split served the army of kids that clamored for a juicy piece. Storytellers surrounded them with the buzz of conversation as they shared embellished tales. It didn't matter what the ages were. Confidantes came in all

years and sizes. A grandmother spoke of a secret she had
harbored all her life with a granddaughter, a father told his son
of a tale from his youth, and friends of all ages shared smiles,
laughs and their life. It was a magical evening.

Love. It's hard to define. It's one of those things you
just know when you love someone. The picnic was a reunion
of family. If you were in this church you were considered
family.

But families, even the best have their tug of war. When
the band stopped for a break, Clarence and Jackie had to
socialize. It would be presumed improper if they didn't tend
to say hello to all the kin and the kindred. That's when they
sometimes got the call of the wild.

"Clarence, you's got to help us out here." The young
teen's eyes were more emphatic than his voice.

Clarence sipped on his beer. He had been called out to
flex muscle between the oldsters and the youngsters. He was
in the middle chronologically and physically. Somehow that
fact appeared to equate fairness and the wisdom of Solomon.
Clarence possessed something all men crave. He had
garnered the respect of every man, woman, teen and child
because he was in the eyes of the community, a success.
Clarence broke ground. He was their Jackie Robinson, and
who wouldn't want to be that?

"Tell 'em. Ain't nothin' wrong with what we doing." A
youthful Turk tilted his head to indicate the divide between
young and old.

Clarence thought it best to keep to himself that which
he clearly heard in his head, "Ah, the oldsters." An angel on
the shoulder of Clarence, whispered, "Tread lightly Clarence,
tread lightly. They're your ancestors."

"Seems like you the deciding factor son." Clarence loved being called "son" by one of the oldsters, be it man or woman.

And then the voice of God erupted as his mother Diedre said her peace. "My boy, tell these kids that dem riots and the looting was wrong, dead wrong, no matter what."

Clarence took a deferential deep breath. "Now, Mama, though I admit the riots was awful, these kids had enough. We all had enough. Maybe they felt they had to use other means of standing up."

Mama Diedre floated into shock. She was certain her flesh and blood would reason with the reasonable.

"Sounds like we won the deciding vote," oozed a Turk with a great big smile.

"Not so fast." Clarence whirled like a top confronting MR. SMILE. "Although you did stand up, you weren't heard."

"The country heard us loud and clear Clarence." If they didn't say it all together in unison, which would have happened had this been a cartoon, it was clearly mirrored in their eyes.

"Now, now, hear me out young men. You weren't heard 'cause nothing changed. All you - well maybe not you - (it was a Solomon smart moment) did was support the stereotype that all we," Clarence in a Heil-Hitler sweeping arc movement of his arm continued, "do is commit criminal acts. And that means that we as a people won't never, never, never, move forward."

An old-timer smiled. "He's playing it safe."

"You can't have it both ways Clarence," rang out a timbre of youthful voices frustrated that when ancestors are involved they can't win.

Right on cue, in an effort to save her man, Jackie smartly appeared. "Baby, you gonna sit hear jabbering or you going to go jammin' with me."

Clarence owned their respect but Jackie had their love. It was a great combination - respect and love.

Clarence peppered their retreat with a final comment looking for laughs, giggles and aw-shucks. "One last piece of advice kids (he pronounced it with affection) - always, always respect your elders."

Diedre's smile returned to her face. She felt fortified.

* * *

The glow of fireworks reflected off the windshield of the Chief's car as John and his trusted Sanchez - Charlie, drove back to their house. "Their house" was central command for nine other houses that made up the 5th Battalion, 150 men strong; a large district of industrial pristine parks encircled by anything but pristine edifices, the slums of the *West Side*. When you lived in "the house" you got the best of everything and the worst of the wrath when the shit hit the fan. When the Chief, a dago, no less, lived in your house, you were at the nerve center, the epicenter, ground zero. Some days were good and some were just fucking awful.

A dispatcher's crackle broke the silence. "Truck 17 rolls to Engine Company 27 for coverage. It's a trash can fire that's died out."

Static crackled in the Chief's car only to leave the trailing transmission of two words... "copy Chief?"

John picked up the mic off the dashboard. "Copy the move." The Chief returned the mic to its clip. "Sucks working the fourth." That became a painfully apparent premonition when the trashcan had the audacity to reignite.

The tale of the trash can fire spread like wild fire. Everyone next to the sound of his master's voice flowing on the waves of Chicago Fire Department radio land heard distinctly the request by a fireman albeit a rookie to his chief, "Clear to go?" A pause of silence was followed by the words, "copy Chief?"

As a result a short ditty rang out now and then among the men, "When Beriso clears an alley, trash cans rally, so let's toast a nip or two for our Chief officer in blue, big bad Blackie Beriso."

The Chief never flinched so much as a twitter. When he walked in on the men in the kitchen of "his house" singing the damn ditty. Every man froze and in-step shared a collective soul-piercing look. You know that look. You've witnessed it yourself when Mickey Mouse played the apprentice wizard to that gnarly looking Grand Wizard? Remember how Mickey blows control of the magic of the Grand Wizard's hat and sorrowfully sets sights for a "sea" of troubles. Remember that? If you do you're older than you look, yet have the wonder of the child. If you haven't seen it, get or rent yourself a copy of Disney's fabulous Fantasia; served with buttered popcorn and the psychedelic de jour of the day.

Beriso knew the cold blue words and sang them that way. Within moments a transformation of Mickey Mouse whacked wizard like eyes smoldering a look of utter astonishment glowed in the room. When "da Chief" finished with his Caruso like delivery of the "Beriso to the alley dittie due" he shot a look back at every Mickey Mouse eye in the room.

"I know what I heard. Our radio had static. Mac'll tell you but my word ought to be good enough. My response that night was, 'Copy move,' ...not 'copy approve.'"

For those who don't know the difference, it's chasms. "Copy move," merely meant acknowledgement of a move from a house to the theater of the fire.

When an officer uttered the command, "Copy approve," it granted permission to an underling to take an action.

Would a chief with that much experience really release a rookie, no less from the scene of a trash fire? It's one of the first things you learn on the CFD; never trust a fire to truly die. When you think it's dead, make damn sure and if necessary give it more water.

A lot of crazy things happened on that Fourth of July, but it was highly unlikely that the Chief would pull a rookie mistake.

The Chief and his Sanchez had run into a drunk. Actually the drunk fell from a raised sidewalk set high above the pavement of a viaduct roadway onto the red car in transit. The drunk slithered and slid across the hood as startled, shit-in-my-pants Mac, slammed on the brakes.

The drunk didn't feel a thing and the car had somehow miraculously escaped the scrape of a bum falling from the sky.

The black bum toppled off the car, but only after it had ceased motion...it was only then when the bum fell off the hood.

Beriso was in no mood. "Clean yourself up and get the fuck out of here!" John had to pull himself away. "Geez you reek of booze, bad booze at that."

The black bum cried. "Help me. I need some help man."

Mac stepped out of the car and heard the bum's plea repeated, "Help me please." Ever the Sanchez to John's Quixote, Mac called an audible.   "Want me to call for an ambulance Chief?"

"Nah, he ain't worth it."

Mac loved his partner. He had such heart. Mac hated his partner. He could be so cold, and heartless at times. It depended on the day. On this Fourth of July, that stupid little song burdened the Chief and so anyone in his way got the worst of his disposition.

As to the ballad, it wasn't long before the ditty became a burden borne by the rookie.

After all, this wasn't the first time a rookie asked to be cleared "toot suite" from the scene of a trash fire. It never failed, they all made that mistake. The rookies had too much of a good thing on their fire fighter minds. They possessed bountiful bodies that yearned for what young studs all think is their forte – sex.   It was good to be young but sometimes youth lacked the focus that came with age, and for a fire fighter, making that kind of faux pas could prove deadly.

———

133

*"All of that is true,' responded Don Quixote, 'but we
cannot all be friars, and God brings His children to
heaven by many paths: chivalry is a religion, and there
are sainted knights in Glory.'*

*Yes,' responded Sancho, 'but I've heard that there are
more friars in heaven than knights errant.'*

*That is true,' responded Don Quixote, 'because the
number of religious is greater than the number of knights.'*

There are many who are errant,' said Sancho.

*Many,' responded Don Quixote, 'but few who deserve to
be called knights."*

Miguel de Cervantes Saavedra, *Don Quixote*

CHAPTER FIFTEEN

BOIL OVER

The day after the Fourth was a drag. People were cranky. Many wanted, some expected it their inalienable right as Americans to a fifth-of-July and maybe even a sixth. That was the trouble with Americans, then, and now; they expected too much.

It was the kind of day that was perfect for a fight, if you could only see it coming. Joe and Vince collectively and individually lacked that ability. "Man, I picked up a lot from that album Clarence gave me," Joe said.

They were at the plant, in the locker room, getting ready to start the day. Vince rolled his eyes. "What? You mean that Tony Williams guy? What do you get from that kind of music?"

"Everything. That guy's got some tasty licks - rudiments I've never heard of, never dreamt of but can now see so clearly. I mean, hear so clearly. I hear it. For the first time, Vince, I really hear it. And not the way I'd play it but the way I wish I could play it, if I could only think it up. But the good news is I can play those chops. Do you know what that means?"

For the first time in a long time, the siblings connected, really connected. They were brothers. Vince was touched that Joe shared something that intimate. Joe just wanted so badly to have a brother; not a sibling who acted like a big brother, constantly checking his progress in life, but a flesh and blood brother to confide in. Why does that, not, click very often in life?

That fifth of July tension crackled in the air with ignition. From another side of the locker room came a challenge.

"You know, that's the problem with you white boys. Always trying to take what we got. Why don't you keep your stocks and bonds and leave the bongo playing to us?"

Fred stared at Vince; he peered at Joe to respond.

"I'm not trying to take from you. I'm trying to learn from you." Joe amazed even himself with that.

Vince, amazed himself with his rat-a-tat response that followed Joe's diplomatic approach. "Why would we want anything you have?" Vince's facial movements broadcast how he was feeling.

"Don't ask me. Ask Elvis that question." Cedric had had enough of the white boy's assertion that he and his kind wanted nothing from blacks.

Joe and Vince both flashed a look of utter confusion at Cedric. He continued. "Yeah, Elvis the pelvis. Shit he stole everything he knows from Jackie Wilson."

"Who's Jackie Wilson?" Vince asked even though he knew who Jackie Wilson was. That pissed off Fred.

"Proved my point." Fred wasn't about to give an inch. Of course the white boy would say that to enrage but Fred forced Vince to engage when he replied matter of fact. "Nobody gives a damn about Jackie Wilson, the real king of Rock 'n Roll."

Vince made it worse. "Jackie Wilson who?" Vince could give a shit about color. It didn't matter if you were white, black, red or yellow. There were just some things that you didn't take from anyone. Who the hell did they think they were to butt into a private conversation? That was so raw. Raw turned to rage and rage engaged four boys into combat.

Fred slammed his locker as he pushed his face into that of Vince. Some would later say that Vince shoved Fred. Others thought Fred had started it. Did it really matter? The die had been cast. "The entire world's a stage, and all the men and women merely players..." aptly covered Cedric and Joe. They were Fred and Vince's wingmen. So they fought too!

The banging in the locker room caught the attention of Clarence and the 'old man.'   Dane opened his window scowling the horizon to find the rumble. If there was one thing he didn't want in his factory it was violence. Violence could lead to a sheer riot and the boiling point had already been passed a long time ago in 1968.

"What the hell's going on in here?" Clarence was livid.

The boys stopped in their tracks. They were facing a lion with its mane full, warning them to beware of their own mortality.

He repeated it.   "I said what the hell's going on in here?"

Fred didn't give a shit. He was sadly disappointed in Clarence, a man he had at one time admired.   "Nothing that we can't handle."

"Well, 'nothing you can't handle' had better come together, cause you, and you and you and yes you are slowing down my lines." Clarence looked into the eyes of each of them.   "And I take that personal, real personal, cause that effects my bottom line. You dig?"

With heads lowered the four culprits exited the locker room. Clarence followed them out with his eyes when he saw the Chief in civilian clothes come into his frame of view. Clarence knew that he had seen it all. There was no spinning this one with Dane. Clarence would have to stick to the script, just the way Shakespeare might have written it and the world knew it at this moment to be.

It was the look. The Chief need not say a word. He didn't have to. Clarence knew he was screwed. What the hell was the Chief doing here?

"Chief, can I help you?"

"I don't know." Beriso looked everywhere but into his eyes.

Clarence waited.

"I'm here for an inspection of the plant for Mercury Insurance. It's my second job."

"Oh." Clarence didn't know whether to wait or not.

"Dane suggested that you serve as my guide through this plant, but maybe under the circumstances it's better that I go off on my own. I'd hate to take you from your pressing duty as foreman and man in control of the floor of this plant."

It was the condescension that Clarence hated. The men were no better than the boys.

*

An engine cranked as the shift came to an end. Workers exited Anderson, Inc. Joe and Vince were the only white faces in a sea of black ones. But the face of Lucille stood out from all the rest as she sat behind the wheel of her pink '57 Cadillac convertible parked alongside the curb as it cranked and cranked. The cranks caught the ears and eyes of both young men. Vince parted company with Joe and headed straight for the damsel in distress.

"What's the problem?"

"I can't seem to get my car started." Lucille cranked it again, resurrecting an engine struggling to turn over. Lucille stopped when she saw it was one of the white boys that came to her aid. *That might be a bit dangerous for the boys and for me.*

Vince nodded to the hood. "May I open her up?"

Lucille panicked. *How do I answer without it sounding rude or friendly?* Within seconds she was composed and only then did she answer, "If you think it will help."

That was the perfect answer. No one could cast a stone at her for that turn of a phrase. Vince cracked the hood open. Lucille exited and joined him under the shade of that big pink Cadillac hood.

"Got a pencil?"

She didn't expect that but you'd never know it. Like a fine instrument, her voice always played a sureness of tone. "Sure do."

Lucille stuck her head into the driver's door window to retrieve her purse that had slid towards the opposite door. Lucille had to reach through the window, which extended her butt, a very fine caboose it was. The men noticed and the women noticed the men noticing. Everyone wondered, "What the hell is she doing fraternizing with them damn white boys?"

The show got better.

Lucille retrieved her purse, aware that she had been noticed. She could care less. Why should she? No one in the factory liked her. She had been cast into caste. There were the whites. There were the blacks. Mulatto wasn't a step up for either side of the black-and-white-white-and-black divide, so that put her into a caste all her own.

The whites of her eyes popped when she faced a solidly built attractive white man who had disrobed his shirt, handing it to Joe, who should have been pissed but wasn't. The pencil fell from her hand. "Oh, I'm sorry."

"Not a problem." Vince grabbed the pencil off the ground. He unscrewed the air filter canister and set it aside. Using the pencil as a wedge, he reached into the engine and jammed the carburetor's choke plate. It was the reach that the women noticed and the men noticed the women noticing. Vince's muscles flexed and glistened under the hot sun as he worked that pencil while Lucille returned to the driver's seat and on Vince's cue cranked the engine. The engine sputtered, then erupted as the jammed open butterfly wedges of the choke plate sucked more air and triggered an explosion.

After her engine started, Lucille clapped with excitement.

Vince put his shirt back on.

"Hop in. I'll give you guys a lift to the bus stop."

Joe wanted to say, "We don't want to be a burden." He politely kept his mouth shut. Vince said something similar for both of them.

"It's the least I can do" smiled Lucille lusciously with those big brown eyes.

How do you refuse? They didn't dare.

Vince rode shotgun as Joe rode in the back.

When appropriate, Vince breathed in a glance of Lucille. It was hard to ignore; her scent was intoxicating.

Lucille chuckled nervously, reacting to Vincent's stare. "What?"

"Nothing." Vince blushed. "You smell nice."

"And you're smooth." Lucille farding as she drove, filled her lips with deep passionate red gloss.

Joe smirked. A girl, a very attractive girl had just paid his big brother the ultimate compliment.

Vince shied from Lucille. She smiled at him to get him back. "It's Idole de Lubin. Worn by the Empress of France in the 18th century. Pierre-Francouis Lubin was a genius. I hope to someday follow in his footsteps."

"Do you speak French?"

"Que l'a donné loin?"

Vince and Joe looked perplexed.

"Que l'a donné loin?" is French for 'what gave it away?'

Vince smiled reacting to her non-question-question. "Hmm, could it be the way you articulated the name of your perfume?" Vince was proud of his enunciation of 'articulated.'

Joe had sat quiet as a mouse for long enough. "How'd you learn French?"

"It was natural. My mom's French."

"But how could you be French?" Vince's face displayed his naivety. For that reason, and only for that reason, she didn't take offense.

Lucille returned his question with a pained look. "I just am. I'm a symbol of blind love. My father was colored, my mother a French immigrant, originally from Pa-ree."

Both boys looked lost.

"You know, pear-ris ...the capitol of France...Paris.

"Oh yeah," Joe voiced acknowledgement for both brothers. "Was your?"

Vince silenced Joe with his look. *No more questions!*

"He died last winter." Lucille returned her concentration to the traffic around them as she drove.

The brothers said it in harmony. "Sorry."

"Can't say I was surprised. Cancer's common among musicians."

Lucille noticed, in her rear view mirror, a quizzical look on Joe's face. "How come?" he asked.

Lucille turned her head slightly behind her to make eye contact with her back seat passenger. It was brief but long enough to melt Joe with the sight of those big brown luscious eyes. "Ever been inside a Blues club?"

Joe shook his head no.

Lucille waited. "You deaf Joe?" I said, 'Ever been inside a Blues club?'"

Joe realized that Lucille couldn't have seen his head shake with her eye on the road. "Sorry about that. I shook my head no."

"No?" Lucille looked over at Vince. "And how about you?"

"It's our old man." Vince needed to blame someone. He didn't want to appear unsophisticated.

Lucille saw through the ruse. "Well, if you had been, you'd know it's like sticking your head in a chimney all day." Lucille could see that her passengers were lost. "I'm talking about the smokiness of a Blues club. There's lots of smoke. Some scientists think that cigarette smoke causes cancer."

Both young men nodded as if they knew all along what this sophisticated young woman meant.

Joe ended his nodding with, "What did he play?"

"Piano mainly. But he could play virtually any instrument. He had to, to last in the entertainment business. Oh my God how he loved the bluessssssss."

Vince was in love with the way she stretched the word Blues. "Me too."

Lucille smiled with sunlight streaming sweetly on her face. "Then you'd love New Orleans. That's where I'm from."

"Really. Ever hang out on Bourbon Street?" Joe's utterance received a wrathful look from Vince. *Why couldn't little brother live the life of a quiet duckling.*

"Practically grew up on Bourbon. My parents met at the club, 500 Club Bourbon. My mom worked there as a waitress. They were as the saying goes, a match made in heaven."

Joe could care less what Vince expected from him. This woman was intriguing and screw Vince for suggesting non-verbally that Joe shut up. "Bet you knew all the Blues greats." Joe continued. He knew a bit about Blues - more than enough not to embarrass himself, something Vince couldn't guarantee if his life depended on it.

Lucille turned the car onto a street headed directly into the western sun. She was aglow like an angel. "Yeah I knew a number of Blues men. More than I'd like to have met. Many of them are here in Chicago. You can see them on Record Row St. - 12th and Michigan."

Lucille could see it in their eyes. "What, you guys don't know about 12th and Michigan?"

"The south side?" Joe sheepishly sighed. "I only wish."

Lucille shrugged in shocked disbelief.

Vince decided to take control of the conversation. "What brought you to Chicago, Lucille?"

"My aunt lives here. She talked my mom into moving here after my father passed away. A new beginning, if you will."

Lucille pulled an 8-TRACK out of the glove compartment and popped it into the player mounted under the dash. Junior Parker's "Pretty Baby," filled the car.

"Junior Parker!" Joe was sure of it.

"Yep. You do know your blues." Her compliment certified Joe's musical genius (or so Joe thought). "My dad's on this jam."

"Wow." Joe's wow was justified. He not only loved Lucille's look but now revered her for having a celebrated father.

Lucille could feel Vince's disconnect. "You into Blues, Vince?"

"Vince thinks Blues is for losers." Joe wasn't about to share his newfound glory with anyone, including his brother.

"I never said that Joe." Vince softened his look as his eyes focused on Lucille. "Contrary to my brother's opinions, I like Blues." Vince turned to Joe and mouthed the words, "You're dead." Joe puckered up to tease him. Lucille noticed the exchange, smiled and shook her head.

———

CHAPTER SIXTEEN

GREEN EYES

Cheesy! That's what that was.
The nerve of that copper, who was he to flirt with Gina and actually get her to laugh?

Beriso's thoughts frothed with envy as he sat and sipped a steaming hot cappuccino coffee at Gina's counter. Gina made cappuccino only for the Chief. Often asked by others to make it for them, Gina remained steadfast in her vestal virgin devotion to her sole cappuccino soul.

Patrick, the police captain, leaned over the counter and kissed Gina. What was worse in John's mind was that she kissed **him** back.

And that **him** wasn't the Chief, whose loins burned for Gina from the moment he saw her. Even when a man loves his wife, there's always that unattainable single woman's smolder that leaves a man wanting more. That revelation may bode badly for man but it's one giant leap for mankind to admit truth rather than concoct fiction. Men are men. And before society condemns them, it must be accepted that their roving eyes have kept the species alive.

Captain Patrick noticed the Chief and waved - impervious to Beriso's head-over-heels affection for Gina.

Beriso waved back. He'd be damn if he gave Patrick the satisfaction.

Gina parted from **him** as he left for his day. She returned behind the counter. "Chief, you done for the day?"

This was more like it. The Chief had her attention. "No, I'm now on Mercury's time. But before I left the firehouse, I got a call from Gloria. The boys forgot their lunches. Could you make a couple of beefs, juicy, with sweet peppers. I'll have a CFD driver pick them up about 11:50 and deliver them to the boys."

"Eleven-fifty...okay." Gina wrote 11:50a on a white bag with a small notation of "2 jcy/swtp," next to the time. She turned away from the Chief to hang it on an order clip that hung above the phone for pick-ups. When she turned back towards the Chief he handed his green-eyed beauty a fin from his wallet to cover the order. Gina protested that it was too much. "Chief, you've got change coming."

"Keep the change. I appreciate the service."

"So are we inspecting for Mercury Insurance again?" She knew from his eyes the answer was yes. "You ever rest Chief?"

Beriso snickered. "I should be asking you that."

Gina shook her hair, her long flowing silky hair. "Point well-taken Chief."

Gina took the carafe off the burner and refilled John's cup with regular coffee. John noticed it wasn't cappuccino even if Gina missed it.

"I commend you Chief. You risk your life every day. I don't know anyone who'd want to be in your shoes."

"Someone's got to do it." The praise had rid the Chief of his resentment for the botched refill.

"And those riots, my God. I don't know how we overcome this."

John nodded as he sipped on his coffee.

"Jimmy and I used to serve people of color all the time. Good, hard working people. Now they no longer come. Why?" Gina looked into his eyes for a truthful answer.

"It's all for the best. There's an awful lot you don't know about them colored, Gina."

"Oh, and I suppose you're got them all figured out."

The Chief stirred some cream into his coffee. He did the same thing when Gloria bitched. All women bitched and when they bitched their eyes burned bright with their color, in this case, green.

The Chief stopped stirring. "You witnessed the riots. You were lucky they didn't rob you."

Gina put the carafe down on the counter and grabbed from beneath it a shotgun. She raised it enough so that only the Chief could see it. "Jimmy had this in case we were ever in any danger but he never tied it to a color."

"Shit, put that-a-way before you hurt yourself."

Gina put it away. "You think I don't know how to use it? Jimmy taught me and I'm a damn good shot if I say so myself, and I do."

The Chief cocked his head back, surprised by a side of Gina he had not seen before. "Let me tell you something Chief. I'm a big girl and I know how to take care of myself. I don't need a man even if I might want a man. Besides you're taken."

That last comment threw the Chief for a loop. Gina had thought of him as a possible suitor. "Yeah I'm taken but don't you be taken in by that playboy."

At that moment Gina's son chased her daughter with flour. Gina shook her head, delighted at the scene. She loved to see her children acting silly. It got her to forget that the husband she loved, Jimmy, had died suddenly, leaving her alone. The void made her cry. Jimmy was the love of her life, a great guy that anyone would be lucky to know. Her departed Jimmy was cordial, warm, and delightfully funny with a great laugh and a loyal devoted lover and husband. Gina considered Jimmy her best friend in life and she missed her friend. But life moves on and Gina longed for the touch of a man. That sounded selfish even to Gina, but the human side of her knew that she needed more than just to live for their kids. Jimmy would have wanted the same for his Gina.

So, if she had to live, she wanted to live life to its fullest. You can't do that without love. To do so is sad. So she needed to nip this obsession by the Chief in the bud. He may have been one of her favorite customers but that's all it would ever be.

"I'm touched by the concern Chief, but make no mistake about it, me and my kids, we're a package. Any man who shows interest knows that. So lose the growl over Patrick."

Gina moved slowly down the counter towards the kitchen double doors. She delivered the knockout punch. "C'mon Chief, it's a new day, it's sunny, at least for me and for you it should be, Gloria treats you like a king, she adores you."

The Chief's growl grimaced into a smile reflected back at him by Gina as she swung open, with her back, the double doors to the kitchen, ready to disappear. "For crisake it's early Chief." John thought Gina was referring to her relationship with Patrick when he heard that alluring accented sound of English with an Italian influence that Gina would revert to now and then, "Ah marone! It's only eight-a forty-nine."

* * *

A CFD red chief's car pulled up in front of the factory. The driver parked it on the apron to the entrance.

Reggie stood by the open bi-fold doors to Anderson, Inc. as he dragged on a smoke. He approached the uniformed driver.

"You know you can't park there."

The white CFD driver in the red car was not about to take guff from an uppity nigger. The fireman reached through the window and flipped a switch. Immediately the factory became awash in red strobe light radiating from the revolving bubble sitting atop the fiery car.

Everyone in the plant noticed the white CFD driver even if they didn't hear him say, "I can now, fire department business. Where can I find Joseph and Vincent Beriso?"

Part of Reggie wanted to tell whitey to go "fuck-off." But a deathly pale came over him instead as a flash of a bad memory struck him. He recalled the lone military officer exiting his car on the street where Reggie lived. When one of the kids told the officer he couldn't park there due to a hydrant, the soldier replied, "Oh, but I can. Army business." And then he heard the man quiz the kids with, "Where can I find Reginald Simmons?" Nobody called him Reginald unless it was something important. That cold day in January, the officer informed him that his son had died during the Tet Offensive on New Year's Day, 1968.

He wondered if the white CFD driver in the red car had come to tell the boys that their father had died in a fire. Reggie would feel like an asshole if he interfered with that; so he turned back to the opening of the plant and yelled in, "Vince and Joe Beriso, c'mere!"

The driver returned to his red car and retrieved through the window on the passenger side a white bag. Upon arrival of Vince and Joe he handed it to Vince.

"Your dad asked me to deliver some beefs from Gina's. They're both with sweet peppers." Vince and Joe smiled *good fortune*.

In unison they said, "Thanks."

"Thank your old man and try not to forget your lunch next time."

Reggie found the entire exchange incredible. He muttered low enough but loud enough to be heard by the driver. "Fire department business, my ass."

The driver ignored the remark. He returned to his car. He didn't need to answer, and so he chose not to. He left with the bubble flashing.

Vince and Joe looked at each other. They were excited. The peanut butter sandwiches that had been their daily fare couldn't hold a candle to the succulent spices of a juicy Chicago style Italian Beef.

The lunch horn sounded; machines powered down. The boys turned back to the factory to find a sea of angry black faces staring at them.

Faye approached Vince and Joe as Reggie and others closed in on the boys. She was enraged. "Not only are you two having beefs for lunch--

Reggie interrupted her. "Something we'd sure love to have but can't for fear of losing our life by the Italian punks who control the viaduct."

Faye cut Reggie off. "How privileged are you two? You rate a special delivery from your daddy's department because you forgot your lunch. Wish we had that safety net. We'd just go hungry."

Clarence emerged from the shadows of the factory convinced he'd have to intervene when he heard Joe propose a novel idea. "You want beefs? We'll go and get you some providing you pay for them."

Vince was as surprised as Clarence. "We will?" Joe elbowed Vince. "Ouch," Vince winced. "Yeah, we will. Whoever wants one, put in."

"Yeah," Joe added, "and don't shortchange us, because Vince and I ain't got it to cover it."

Workers closed in, but this time with an air of excitement rather than with resentment. The mood shifted that quickly. Jimmy & Gina's beefs tasted that good.

Faye huffed. "Y'all gonna just let them play you like that?"

Faye's entreaties were ignored as factory workers offered their two-dollar bills for a bit of culinary paradise.

"Don't miss my order!"

"One at a time." Vince needed a pen and something to write on. He thought of using the white bag.

"Hey, wait a minute!" Clarence boomed.

A deathly pale came over the crowd turned mob. They were sure Clarence would nix the offer.

"Get a hold of yourselves!" Clarence handed his clipboard and a pen to Vince. "Can't just shout out orders. Gotta write 'em down."

The mob reverted to a crowd, smiling and laughing at the unexpected answer. Vince used the clipboard to support the white bag. He wrote as fast as he could on the bag - while Joe collected the money, jamming a hundred one dollar bills into his two front pockets. The tops of some of the George Washington's could be seen.

The boys headed off with the cheers of their co-workers...with the exception of Faye and her pregnant co-worker Sandra. Vince and Joe underwent a transfiguration. They were in their own little trance of glory much like the characters in the *Wizard of OZ*. In this case they were off to see the wizard of Italian beefs with a request to get a whopping fifty. The depth of this order was overwhelming for a couple of strangers in a land that was not theirs.

* * *

Gina's diner was packed with a lunchroom crowded with Caucasians. The boys approached the counter. Gina, a bit spent, finished serving a customer. She greeted the boys at the far end of the counter. "What can I do for you young gentlemen?" She paused as she studied the boys. "Are you the Chief's sons?"

The boys were surprised by that question. "How'd you know?" Joe replied.

"Well, for starters you both look a bit like your dad and you're holding one of my white bags marked with my handwriting." Gina pointed to what the boys had never noticed. "See that's my code for two juicy beefs with sweet peppers. Next to it is the pick-up time. I only had one at 11:50 a.m. and that was yours. You did get your delivery, didn't you?"

"Oh yeah, thanks. Joe nodded his head towards his brother, "Vince and I are back for more."

"And you are?"

Vince realized his little brother didn't get Gina's drift. "He's Joe, the baby of the family."

Joe hated hearing that moniker which his brother loved to throw around. He was envious of Vince's stature as the older son, which in an Italian family was tantamount to being the crowned prince.

Gina laughed. "Don't you worry about being the bambino. You're a cute one!" Now it was Vince who was envious.

Gina liked that she could turn a head, even a young man's when it came to her charms. "You liked them that much."

Gina loved when people loved her food, especially the beefs. That was a credit to her Jimmy. He tried spice after spice after spice ad infinitum before he *settled* on the sauce. *Settled* was the only way to describe it. In fact, Jimmy continued to fiddle with the sauce after that but found he could never beat the sauce he *settled* on.

"We liked them so much that we want fifty more!" Vince surprised even himself with the exclamation in his voice.

Vince's order caught the attention of every patron in the restaurant as the clientele collectively became silent to hear.

Gina couldn't help but notice that all eyes were on her. "You're kidding?"

"No, I'm dead serious," replied Vince. "How fast can you get together fifty Italian beefs?" Vince being an Italian-American knew how to say Italian without putting an eye in it.

"That's one hundred dollars worth of food boys. That's not something you kid about." Gina drew the line on practical jokes. She couldn't afford to be the butt of a teenager's joke.

Joe emptied his pockets on the table for all to see. He stacked the bills neatly into ten columns of ten George Washington's.

Gina was amazed but without further reflection, scooped up the money. "Okay, fifty beefs ah comin' up." Gina turned back to the kitchen. "Mama, prega di inserire carne in più al calore (put extra beef on to heat). Abbiamo ottenuto cinquanta (we got fifty)."

From the back of the kitchen the word "Cinquanta" with a question mark in the voice erupted.

"Si Mama. Cinquanta - fifty." Gina moved into the kitchen to help her mother complete the order.

This was a good day for Jimmy & Gina's, or rather just "Gina's." Gina had to make the break and that meant everything including the name of *their* restaurant. Things had changed. The business was no longer "their's", but "her's" with all the responsibility that came with that...the bills, the care of their kids, the running of the restaurant; life itself. She had been a widow. She wanted to love again and more importantly to be loved. Isn't that what every woman wants? Frankly, isn't that what every man wants? She wanted what Jimmy would have wanted her to want. He would have wanted her to be happy. That's the kind of man Jimmy was in the flesh or in the spirit.

The receipts on this day overshadowed *their* best day ever together. At the moment it was *her* best day - alone, for now. But "best" days are often brutal. To get out the order, man the register, take the new orders and help Mama in the kitchen make fifty sandwiches quickly while keeping them warm without overcooking was a trick that Jimmy had taught her. She in turned passed that on to her Mama, a great cook notwithstanding her novelty with the restaurant business. Someday Gina hoped to pass her place on to *their* kids, providing they would want to carry on the business. Dino and Mia would always be *their* kids no matter what Tom, Dick or Juan she made a bed with.

———

CHAPTER SEVENTEEN

OLD FEARS DIE HARD

While the clock went tick-tock at Gina's it also did the same at Anderson, Inc. where Faye noticed the quiver in the eyes of her co-workers. They had given two white boys a hundred dollars of their hard earned money. Who *was to say* whether they ran off or not? It was Faye...Faye was to say and say it she did, loud enough for others to hear. "Probably run off with y'alls money. Now how stupid do you feel."

Reggie didn't care. He'd had it with Faye's surliness. "Shut-up. Shut the..." Reggie stopped short of setting off a nuclear blast. Faye was ready.

Clarence's chest tightened. He moved immediately to cool things off. "Nobody ran off with anything. C'mon let's treat each other with respect, and," he paused for effect, "if you can't do that, then keep your mind on your task."

Clarence walked that fine line between parties at odds with one another. He delicately blamed both parties but in such a way that neither party felt abandoned. Each party heard Clarence take their side. That's why Clarence was 'the man.'

The only worker on the plant floor that could distinguish the subtlety of Clarence's words was Diego. That was his little secret. It made him proud.

* * *

It took a full twenty minutes to complete the order. Gina felt bad, but there was little she could do. It was at the peak of lunchtime when hunger pisses people off and customer demands must be met. There's a mean streak to the hour because the anticipation of food, like sex, sometimes makes people crazy.

So it was only natural that she threw an extra one in for love, "cause I make you wait." The bonus beef was capped off with a smile and a cock of the head that males, no matter what the age, found appealing.

That got a testosterone rush from her newfound young beaus who had their father's Roman blood flowing through their veins. Like dad, like son; the Beriso males with frustrated heads fantasized fornicating with the green-eyed Italianette.

"Thanks." Vince grabbed at both bags and tried to flee but Gina wouldn't let go.

"Tell your friends at the factory, they're welcome anytime."

Joe and Vince squirmed an uneasy glance. Gina noticed the boys' reaction, sighed as her face cut a wry smile of understanding. These young men were expected to move with their sea of humanity, the white folk. She would cover for them as her patrons looked and listened in to why the need for such a large order.

"Let me guess, Dane's got a *board of directors* meeting?" Gina could see the boys didn't get *'board of directors*.' So Ms. Green Eyes tried again. "You know a meeting with his investors."

Vince nonchalantly recovered. "How'd you know?"

Gina glowed, "That's my secret."   The rest of the restaurant returned to life satisfied that they were in the know. Only then did Gina let Vince go.

Vince blasted through the door.   Joe followed a step behind.   They motion-blurred into the shadow of the viaduct with the obscurity of impressionistic art, almost knocking over Gina's beloved bus boy, Mike.   After apologizing to Mike, the boys headed for the bright white light at the end of the tunnel of the viaduct.   A train was rattling overhead so loud that it was uncomfortable to their ears.   They crossed to the other side of the street, the side that Anderson Inc., sat on.

Joe jumped up on the curb with a zip in his step. "It's good we forgot our lunch today."

Vince wasn't so sure.   The only thing he was certain about was that, "I'm sick of Mom's sandwiches."

"No." Joe raised one of the two bags Vince had thrust on him immediately after spinning Mike, like a top.   "I meant *this*." He held up even higher, *this* - his white bag of sandwiches.

"Think it'll make a difference?" Vince needed reassurance.

Joe reassured. "Did you see how excited they were?"

Out of the darkness. "Who's they?"

They had another ninety feet to go before they'd reach the light.

From the shadows lurked a dozen scary looking WOP punks, all built like bricks, wearing blue jeans, leather jackets, chains and slicked hair ala Elvis, none of that Beatle longhaired shit.

Vince took control.   He whispered to Joe, "Let me handle this."

The dozen goons encircled the Beriso's much the way a pride of Lions encircle an Elephant when they take 'em down. The punks held longneck bottles of beer. Some gulped while others smashed the bearer of their beer onto the rubble of their hangout. These were grown, albeit young men, who wasted time away under a viaduct, lost in time. Literally, there were no other restaurants like Jimmy and Gina's.

With the help of their Chicago alderman and five-hundred Washington's under the table, Jimmy and Gina's was somehow grand-fathered out of having to obey an ordinance that demanded an entrance and an exit to all restaurants. For virtually every restaurant in the city, this was a mandatory condition. You could only get into Jimmy and Gina's from the front. That was a given. The restaurant had been sculpted into the construction of a viaduct also with an under the table exchange of green backs. The only difference was the amount.

"I said, 'Who's they?'" Out of the shadow a punk stepped into a stream of light that cracked through a rogue rust hole in the bed of the viaduct above. It was good to be a goon. You were a force to be feared.

A punk, about 15 feet away from the goon spokesman, tossed his bottle onto the rubble and glass exploded into a shower of refracted light bouncing the beam of Mother Sun. Goon-the-spokesman grabbed Vince's white bag of beefs only to have Vince yank it back.

"Hands off. This is Dane's food."

"All of 'em? What for?" The beer bottle-tossing brat demanded to know.

"Dane's got a meeting. His board of directors." Vince was delighted to see that they didn't have a clue. "You know, his investors."

Goon-the-spokesman nonchalantly recovered. "Sure, we heard. Word gets out. We hear everything, you know how it is."

Vince relaxed until beer-bottle-blaster blistered Gooney's ego with, "Nah! Those beefs are for them niggers at the plant, ain't they?"

Vince froze. Joe didn't miss a beat. "C'mon guys, you think Paisans like us would buy anything for those moulies?"

Joe had not only pulled it out of the fire for Vince but also saved face for goon-the-spokesman. What he just did went against his grain, but in this case it was definitely necessary.

Goon recovered once again, smoothly, and nonchalantly. "Leave 'em alone. Can't you see they're one of us?" Goon turned from beer-bottle-blaster, the heir apparent and younger Lion who loved to challenge goon-the-spokesman's hierarchy. "But tell Dane the next time he sends you to Gina's, he'd best pop a few of those beefs our way."

They may have been punks but they *got* the memo watching Mike pull down "Jimmy's" from the signage. It was now just Gina's sans "Jimmy's."

The punks laughed as they dissipated into an abyss of satanic goon darkness, as quickly as they had emerged from it.

Vince and Joe waited as a new day dawned without goons, then split for the light.

"Moulies?" Vince had never heard his brother utter that word.

"Worked didn't it? Not to mention that you, my heroic big brother, fuckin' froze. The next time you leave me hangin' after driving it home with, 'I'll handle this' only to come dangerously close to you killing us...at least have the decency to yell fore!"

* * *

The expectation was unexpectedly excruciating yet exhilarating. With each tick the workers tock'd with anticipation. New questions arose. *Would they be able to bring home that big of an order? Would they get their asses kicked by the goons?*

It's soulful how communal food is and yet it can be so culturally - vastly different. Food was the Alpha and the Omega when it came to the evolution of a species created in part by the codec of cuisine indigenous to a particular region, country, or continent. Food revealed much about the people who cherish the cuisine that tastes so palatable. Food was good. It was also deliciously bad. It didn't matter if you lived in Eden or the West Side of Chicago, human nature necessitated the need to partake of the forbidden fruit, be it an apple or an Italian beef...form didn't matter.

Joe's smile beamed as the boys reached the wide open doors of Anderson, Inc. "Beef's anyone?"

A swarm encircled them as they passed out the verboten manna. The machines whirred in abandonment.

"Gina says you're welcome anytime." Vince missed how incredibly stupid that sounded to the *folks* of Anderson, Inc. Joe grasped the gravitas of his brother's, actually Gina's words, as the pupils of eyes expanded and excreted pitiful looks.

Reggie took mercy on Vince, a young white man who had stuck his neck out. He didn't want anyone rebuffing him with something that might hurt, so he broke the pregnant pause, fully filled by the whir of run-away machines that Clarence either failed to notice or care about. "That's easier said than done but you're too," he pondered '*white*' but said, "young to appreciate the matter. What you did could have been dangerous, so thanks."

The eyes widened with appreciation for Reggie's patience and for what Vince and Joe had done. It hit home that what the boys did could have been dangerous. This was a moment that they all could share and for that reason no one dared move to the confines of the canteen. Each found a spot within steps of where they stood, sat and celebrated with their colleagues their good fortune. Every now and then even a 'colored' deserved a fucking break. They had waited so long to have something so pleasurable denied by whites who hated them yet supplied by those same whites that many had at some point in their suffering collectively agreed to hate.

For all but Faye, it was futile to dislike the Beriso boys yet alone hate them. Quietly keeping it close to her vest, Sandra lost her need to hate them anymore, as *whites* they had stuck their necks out for the Negroes at Anderson, and that was impossible to dismiss. Fred and Cedric were amazed when they took their order. Vince and Joe weren't the kind of *white* guys they knew. So it wouldn't have mattered whether Reggie said anything or not. This one they'd let go. They all knew Vince was utterly naive to the world that a Negro faced in 1968.

The extra beef went to Dane who offered to share half with his secretary Lucille. She politely declined, attentively aware of Dane's cravings. That acuity earned her a salacious reputation with women jealous of her killer looks and Boston coffee-colored skin. Not a bad word was heard from any man when it came to Lucille, just lustful thoughts of a sexual-coitus with the girl in their dreams.

For Lucille, giving up a bite of beef was a win-win. It was pointless anyway; Dane would have been stingy with any split of the beef. She had, this day by the grace of God, cold southern fried chicken in her lunch basket made by her mama that could more than fill the void.

One by one, the whir of machines were silenced, even Faye's, as Anderson employees enjoyed a communal moment of ingesting morsel by morsel, the delectably juicy sandwiches, with savor reserved for fabulous food you can't help but eat passionately. Passion tilts people irrationally.

Clarence finished with reflection. "Vince, Joe. That EYE-TALIAN beef was outstanding. Is all EYE-TALIAN food that good?"

The boys smiled. Everyone smiled.

"So I'd like to show my gratitude by inviting you to my neighborhood for a dinner of soul food. And my guess is that you boys have never had it."

It was an awkward moment for the boys. Shock and awe permeated the plant as the on-lookers wondered, "How would they respond to the invitation?"

"This Saturday. Say eight o'clock?"

The pupils of every eye opened "wide shut! *What could Joe say?* "Uhm, okay."

Vince couldn't believe he heard the word, 'okay.' He directed his look at his brother, "Whoa, Joe! We may not have a car." Vince turned to Clarence and the others. "So we're not sure we can make it."

"Well, think about it and let me know by the end of the week. My wife's a great cook."

A congregation of voices sang different pitches of the word, "Amen." With the help of his wife's culinary skills, Clarence converted many of the doubting Thomases, winning their hearts, minds, stomachs and good will in the hearth of his home. He and his lovely wife shared their family, their hopes, their dreams; that kept him humble, human and a harbinger of what could come if they all worked together.

It was Joe's turn to sound out-of-touch. "Yeah, we'll get back to you on that one Clarence."

The boys, nervous, embarrassed and bashful at that moment sought the solace of each other and the only place they'd find that was on the apron out in front. They needed to regroup to try and understand how their gesture of good will had turned ill. *How the hell do you handle the overwhelming feeling of an out-of-control full-blown vibe?*

The workers left behind slithered around Clarence. Melvyn broke the silence and spoke the unspoken. "What you crazy, Clarence, inviting them white boys to your home for dinner. Those white boys ain't gonna step anywhere near your neighborhood."

"Why not?" Unlike every other person of color breathing in that plant, Clarence believed it could happen.

"Besides, you're Momma will kill you when she finds out." Melvyn's statement launched contagious laughter that spread among the faithful.

Only Reggie dare utter words of change. "I still say, 'Why not?'" But his face said it all.

"Wanna wager on that?" It was one of the troublemakers.

Clarence's blood came to a boil. But he was damned if he'd let anyone feel the heat.

"Two-to-one says they don't." It was the other troublemaker. The fever spread quickly. "I'll give you three-to-one."

"Me too. I'll take that bet."

"Lookie, here, I'll go three-to-one on that. Them white boys ain't going to the South side of Chicago. No way."

Clarence puffed. "I don't gamble."

While the men looked astonished, Faye found her way. "Precious white boys ain't worth the risk, huh, Clarence?"

Clarence wanted to grab the smirk off her face and use it to kill her. "All right. I'll take you on but on my terms, five-to-one action that, we, the boys and I, break bread before midnight on our side of town. I do that, the pot's mine for the taking."

From Elmer, the stuttering, cross-eyed fork-lift driver came, "Five…five…five-to-ah-one…one is a lot of dough. How's we…how's we gonna…gonna know Clarence if they show."

"You'll know. I'll tell you. You do trust me to be honest?"

Reggie grabbed a clipboard and pen from Clarence's desk. He wasn't about to let anyone besmirch Clarence's integrity. This was getting ugly. So he queried, "Who's in?"

In a split-second, they barked out their bets like traders in the pits. Reggie recorded every bark dutifully. He even recorded his own bet. Even though he wanted to believe, he couldn't see them white boys traveling south.

Like the boys, Clarence sought the refuge of the apron. It was stranger than weird; maybe it was a vibe.

* * *

Vince and Joe pushed through their front door, the solace of their home, only to have their father in their face giving them the eye. "Dane told me about the stunt you two pulled today."

John's words slashed into the boys. They froze; their guts eviscerated.

"Since when do we do favors for niggers?" The
harshness stung.

Vince dove under the covers of blame. He was going to
survive the impending onslaught of criticism with a credible
defense.

"Dad, they wouldn't stop bitchin' when we got our food
from the driver." Vince's ploy was met sharply.

"What the hell do you care what they think? They're
niggers."

"What's the big deal?" Joe whined making it abundantly
clear that he considered his old man's thinking as nothing less
than "fucked up." It was inevitable that their antlers would
eventually clash, considering the diverse worlds they lived in.

John could read Joe like a book. He wasn't about to
give his son the satisfaction of rattling the old man. "They can
fetch their own...*he wanted to say fucking* but couldn't... damn
beefs."

"But they'd get clobbered, Dad." Joe was sincere.

Vince and Joe were locked on this. They knew they
had done the right thing, the decent thing by extending
themselves to their co-workers. Vince was determined to
support his little brother even though he hated him for
challenging the old man. *"What the fuck for?"* thought Vince
but he had to give the old man an out to save face and appear
fair. "A bunch of greasers got a hangout outside Gina's.
C'mon, Dad. They're just waiting to clock the colored."

"Those greasers are keeping the niggers in line...you
know, keeping 'em on their side! The way it ought to be!"
John believed in the greasers mission even if he didn't
appreciate the punks.

Joe had it. He bolted up the stairs.

"Where you think you're going?"

Joe turned. He pierced his father's eyes with sadness. "I'm sick of this place!" Joe continued to move up the stairs.

"Get use to that room, smart ass! You'll be seeing a lot of it this weekend. You're grounded!" John, pissed and not satisfied with the charade, lashed out at the only son he could. "That goes for you too, Vince."

Vince was stunned. It didn't seem fair. He tried to be his father's son but he couldn't, not on this. Frankly his father's conduct was - he struggled to find the right word - but the only word that came to his mind was - "racist." Vince was disappointed that his father was no better than Bull Conner. Connor had directed in 1963 the use of fire hoses and police attack dogs in Birmingham against civil rights activists, including black children of the protesters. Even though five years had passed, the raw images were fresh. The New York network newsrooms played it repeatedly during the coverage of the riots of 1968.

———

CHAPTER EIGHTEEN

ONE STEP AT A TIME

The Saturday morning mist sparkled from the splash of the sun's rays. John's uniform bled blue onto the canvas of life as the Chief exited his house and slid behind the wheel of his '68 Impala. Everything was his. He was, after all, Chief.

The boys followed their father's path as Vince rode shotgun and Joe settled into a back seat. Today was an extra day of work with overtime at Anderson. It was a bit of a test. Could Anderson meet the ridiculous deadlines imposed by Marshall Field for production? If production went well, more jobs would be forthcoming making everyone including Dane a bit richer.

"Here's for the streetcar home." John handed each boy a token. John cranked the key. The engine ignited, but father was far from being done. "Remember, in the house after work." Father's eyes meant it.

Joe and Vince both proffered to their father a nod of pure submission. For Vince it was a moment of thanks. *"Thank God Joe at least knows when to shut up."*

As the car entered Chicago's West side in the friendly confines of the 5th Battalion, the boys invariably lost their span of attention. "Hey!" John's shout woke them up, "we're here."

"For how long?" Joe said out of the blue but everyone knew what he meant.

Ah, shit! The little fucker had to challenge the man again. When the fuck was Joe ever going to learn not to fuck with the old man?

"Till I decide to let you off. Rest up for Sunday." John's bark reverberated through the car.

"Why?" Vince suddenly said in a tone that made it clear, a gauntlet had been thrown. It was a vicious cycle that the Beriso men repeated over and over.

John didn't need this. It was a pimple on his ass to take it from the rebellious baby of the house but from his first-born son, it hurt. So the tone turned compassionate.

"Hey, it's our Sunday together with the Cubs and, with dinner, it's a long day."

The tone softened from the boys. "Really?" said Vince. Joe followed. "Who's playing?"

"It's not every day you get two of the greatest ballplayers ever to play the game on the same field. Vince, you know whom I'm talking about?"

Vince and Joe both knew that answer, but it was the older son who got asked. "Willy Mays and Ernie Banks."

John smiled back. Their dysfunction, which none of them would take ownership of, rolled on and on like dice on a crap table seeking the almighty lucky seven

.

* * *

The horn at Anderson, Inc. sounded as the day wound down. The whir of machines collapsed all around them. Vince and Joe would go home without distraction, set on a mission - to please the old man.

"Vince. Vince!" The excitement of Lucille's voice distracted Vince. Vince turned to see a very nattily dressed-for-success Lucille. "Lucille. You look nice!"

Lucille blushed. "My girlfriends and I are going to be at the Kitty Kat Club tonight on Clark Street. I'd love it if you and Joe could join us."

Vince's smile dissipated. "Oh, Lucille. I can't."

The rejection hit Lucille hard but she elected not to share that with Vince. *"It's okay."*

"Wait please. It's not what you think."

Lucille took issue with that. How could a man tell what she was thinking? "Oh and what do I think?" Her retort dripped with the mystique of a woman between fascination and scorn.

Was she being sarcastic? Vince knew his answer would make or break him with this bit of forbidden fruit. He was that attracted to Lucille. "I don't know why I said that? Please forgive me."

The sincerity shook her. Here was a male who actually got it.

"Look, our old man grounded us. We can't leave our house."

Lucille looked shocked. She hadn't expected their limited freedom. She was an adult even though she was younger than the boy Vince.

"Okay?" Vince added, "Now I'm thoroughly embarrassed."

"Don't be." Lucille liked his forthrightness.

"Yeah, we're not on the best of terms with our old man right now. He unloaded on me when Joe gave him lip. It happens all the time and I'm...." Vince stopped.

"What?" Lucille really wanted to know.

"I'm sharing with you the sick dynamic between my father and brother. I often feel trapped in the middle."

Lucille exited the plant with Vince and then turned towards her car. She looked back at Vince. She softened her face into a smile. "Well maybe another time."

Oh my God, what a smile. Captivated by that smile, Vince felt like a pirate who has just uncovered a rainbow filled treasure chest with fifty pieces-of-eight.

As the gifted eavesdropper that Elmer was, the forklift driver had overheard that which Clarence only wished he knew. Vince and Joe weren't going anywhere, let alone a trip to the South Side of Chicago to break bread with Clarence. Now was the time to jack up the bet.

Elmer found Clarence. "Hey boss! The...the guys...and I, I, I, wan...wanna up-the-ante on our bets."

The groundbreaking announcement caught everyone's attention. "What are y'all up to?" Clarence could smell a set-up.

"It's ah, ah, ah, what, what...you, you and your friends aren't up to. I, I, I, say, say...they're def...def...definitely not going to your pad tonight."

Clarence took a good look at all the men waiting anxiously to hear his reaction. He now knew how Christ felt with his fellow man. A few were sincere, but most had the scrutinous heart of a Pharisee. *The best defense is a good offense,* or so Clarence thought. "Now, why in hell would you know that?"

"I..I..I...gots my ways." The forklift driver didn't appreciate Clarence's hubris. *Who the hell do he think he is?"*

Clarence didn't like turning negative but shit, it was the only way he was going to find anything out - so - he snickered, chuckled and laughed at the forklift driver, hoping he would bite.

"I overheard 'em tell Lucille....dat...dat they...they can't leave their house 'cuz...cuz they're grounded."

"Gotcha!" Clarence squeezed out the truth. He shook his head no, for all the adversaries to see. "All bets are final. I'm not taking any more action."

The men were disappointed but not angry. They reserved their anger for the forklift driver who blew it. *How could he fall for the oldest trick in the book?*

Clarence had to take action. If he lost the bet, his wife and mother would send him to hell for being a gambler, no matter what his motive. The road to hell was paved with good intentions.

* * *

Vince and Joe were waiting for a bus when Clarence pulled up. He rolled down the window. "You boys need a lift?"

Vince and Joe, surprised by the offer, were unsure of how to respond. Joe looked for brotherly leadership. That meant Vince.

"No thanks Clarence. Our bus will be here soon enough."

"It might help you guys...get you ready sooner for that trip down to my place tonight." Clarence leaned across the seat and opened an inviting door.

Joe saw Vince's eyes blink. "Yeah, about tonight--

Clarence cut him off. His smile turned serious. "Hop in. We'll talk about it on the way."

But they didn't. They talked about everything from the weather to the Cubs. Clarence felt if he could win them over they'd go. They had to or he was screwed.

When they finally got to the curb in front of the Beriso home, Clarence let them exit with a "Home in no time, guys."

"You two set on directions to my place?"

Joe was just as set to push back. " We'd like to make it, Clarence. Really. We've been trying to tell you that our old man grounded us."

"Aw c'mon guys, if you're scared it's okay to tell it like it is." Clarence felt bad for pulling out that card and playing it. He knew he'd get a reaction.

From a window covered by sheers stood the shadow of Gloria Beriso. She couldn't hear but she could see the animation and intensity in her son's face. Although home alone, she voiced what she thought. "Oh God! What are they doing riding in a car with a colored?"

Vince nudged Joe to notice that just across the street a group of white preteens advanced with rocks in hand.

"Better get out of here, Clarence." Joe's animation was passionate.

"What?" Clarence looked and saw what he had seen so many times before, hate.

A white preteen with a demonic face demanded, "Hey, what's that nigger doing in our neighborhood?"

A second white preteen with an angelic face queried, "You guys know him or something?"

Vince was not going to let these kids threaten him.

"No idiots!"

Clarence perturbed at the Simon Peter betrayal. The cock hadn't even crowed once, locked eyes with Vince. Vince glared back, uncomfortable with his conduct.

Vince screamed. "He's lost asshole. What's it to you?"

Vince's macho ploy failed. The preteens took off throwing rocks at Clarence's car. The side mirror on

Clarence's car shattered. Clarence shielded himself with his left arm as he used his right arm to whip the steering wheel for a getaway.

Clarence looked into his rear mirror and saw angry young white boys hurl their rocks as they screamed epithets filled with hate. He slammed his fist on the dashboard enraged. This was his city too. If he had come in peace, and he had, then he should have been able to choose the time to leave.

Vince and Joe looked at each other resigned and ashamed at themselves and their neighbors.

Gloria saw a blue-cold wind of pain freeze her sons' faces with guilt. They lowered their heads and walked home where they always found comfort from their mother. Gloria knew that better than anyone else. As much as she loved her husband there were days when he could be downright difficult. She would comfort her troubled sons and ask details later.

* * *

A grandfather clock displayed 8:15. The clock kept perfect time with its pendulums visible behind a glass pane in the beautifully polished walnut finished cabinet that housed the mechanism. The clock held court with a majesty that commanded respect. It was the oldest vestige of the Wilson family's heritage from their move to Chicago from the south, some fifty years prior.

Clarence sat at his dining room table miffed at himself as his mother Deidre carried plates from the kitchen, put them on the table and then began to cover bowls of food. "Clarence this food's getting cold. Where are they?"

Before Clarence could utter a word, Jackie at work washing dishes, looked through the pass-through between the kitchen and the dining room at Clarence. "Talk about rude."

"They're probably lost." Clarence didn't know what to say.

"Who are they?" Deidre finished covering the bowls of food. "You never did share that."

"You don't want to know, Mama."

Jackie shifted her eyes from Deidre to Clarence. "You don't want to tell your mother, Clarence?"

Clarence shook his head. He knew when they were ganging up on him. "Two of my employees."

"What?" Deidre didn't hear her son's answer.

Clarence said it louder. "Two of my employees."

"What makes them so special that we got's to slave all day over a hot stove, only to have them not show up." Deidre looked to Jackie, pleased that her daughter-in-law was not pleased with her Clarence.

Jackie was angry with Clarence the moment he told her about the invitation...how hopelessly stupid...and yet...nothing. She was angry. "They're white Mama. Can you imagine that?"

"White? Clarence, you know we ain't never had no white people here."

"First time for everything." Clarence said the unthinkable with a bit of resignation in his voice.

The response amazed Deidre. Her son wanted to implement change, *and that don't come easy.* Deidre stopped judging. She was a mother before anything else. She could feel the hurt in his reply. Jackie noticed as well. Her mother-in-law could still teach a thing or two on how to be a nurturing woman.

She accepted the lesson and whispered his name softly, "Clarence." She caught his disappointed eyes softly as she leaned into the pass through. "Eat. They're not coming."

A flash of car beams bounced off a decorative front room mirror. Clarence rose from his chair, excited as he rushed to peer out the front window. The headlights died. A man and a woman, he had never seen before, stepped out of the car and walked to the three flat across the street.

"Dammit!"

"Taking it kinda hard, ain't you son?"

Jackie entered the living room. She placed her hand on a chair for support. She waited for Clarence to return to his seat. He knew it was coming.

"That's because he's hiding something Mama, what you think it is?"

Deidre wanted no part of this fight but she was intrigued by Jackie's comment. "We're waiting. So is your wife right? Are you hiding something?"

Clarence hated when they double teamed him. It was hard enough for any man to live with one woman but with two it was impossible. He agreed to do it. It was Jackie's idea. With Mama, they could get a home.

Jackie desperately wanted to own a home. When Clarence's father died, a door closed as another opened. They could get a house with Mama's help even if that meant Jackie had to share it with her mother-in-law. She had come to love Diedra in part because she sided more often with her daughter-in-law than she did with her son.

Deidre thought her son lucky to have Jackie, a god-fearing, morally righteous woman that did her share and then some. For Deidre it meant having children in her life again and that for her was sheer joy.

Clarence refused to sugar coat the truth. "I have a bet with the men at the factory."

"Gambling? Don't you know boy gambling's the devil's work?"

Jackie would let her mother be self-righteous. She was interested in the possible damage. "How much was the bet?"

"About a week's pay."

Both Jackie and Deidre sighed heavily throwing their arms up in the air in disbelief.

"That's if I lose."

"If you lose? You see any white boys come through that door tonight?" Jackie put her hand to her mouth trying to catch her breath and stopping herself from saying something irreparable.

"There's still time." Clarence was an eternal optimist.

Diedra dared not say a word. Jackie was on a roll. "And they said with certainty that they were coming?"

"Well...not exactly."

"Not exactly? You mean you had Mama and I slave all day in the kitchen and you knew they might not come?"

Clarence hated the questions.

"What's gotten into you son? Gambling money you know this family needs."

"I know what I'm doing Mama! I *am* the man of the house."

"Man of the house? A man puts his family first." Deidre looked at her son, who suddenly appeared ashamed. "Son, I hate to say this but you've acted like a child."

"Naw, Mama, let Mr. Big Man do what he want. The kids and I won't be around to see it. Excuse me, but I got some packing to do for the three of us." Jackie paused for effect, then telepathed via her eyes a message that was loud and clear. *Do you Clarence take me for a lover or am I just the dutiful wife? Cause if you think that's good enough, it ain't.* Then came the shock pronouncement. "Oh, let me know when my momma and daddy get here. My guess, it'll be fifty minutes - tops, sixty."

———

"There are those who look at things the way they are, and ask why... I dream of things that never were, and ask why not?"

\- Robert Francis Kennedy

CHAPTER NINETEEN

NO MAN'S GROUND

Joe and Vince knelt behind the balusters on the stairs staring into a dark living room with a television transmitting black-and-white images as its sole audience member slept on the couch. A shaft of light glaring from the television illuminated a sound asleep Gloria.

"This is a bad idea," whispered Vince.

Joe sharply whispered back indignantly, "Shut up! You don't have the balls to go. If so, I'll go without you."

"I'm behind you ain't I?"

"Then go Vince." Joe led the way. They tiptoed down the steps, down the hall and out the backdoor.

Joe rushed to lift the garage door as Vince locked up the house. Upon reaching the Bel-Air, Joe slid behind the steering wheel.

Vince ran up to the driver's window signaling no with a wave of his hand. "Don't start it now. We'll push it out."

Joe got out of the car and through the open window began to push and steer. "C'mon Vince, give me a hand here."

United in cause and brotherhood, the boys pushed the Chevy down the driveway in the cover of darkness with the silence of a commando raid.

"Left, left," whispered Vince.

Joe responded to his brother's command by turning the vehicle into the middle of the street.

"Now let's push it down a bit." Joe followed Vince's orders as they pushed the Bel-Air down the street. After they had moved the car four houses down the block, Joe jumped behind the wheel and started the engine. Vince gave his sibling a look, but then jumped in and off they went in cause and brotherhood as one.

* * *

"Put your jackets on." She waited as they followed their mother's directive. "Now your shoes." Jackie finished packing *their* little suitcases which she carried in her right arm while firmly gripping the handle of her satchel as she marched towards the front door with her two little troops. *She loved this man, what was she doing?*

Clarence frightened, pleaded, "Can't we talk about this?"

That's exactly what Jackie wanted but Deidre shot her a look that made it clear how she felt. "*Don't let that man get-a-way-with-it, even if he's my boy.*"

Coldly Jackie pulled the trigger, "I ain't got nothin' to say to you."

Clarence put his hands to his head wrenching the sadness within his grasp. Deidre cried a small tear as she witnessed her son's agony. She resolved to help him even if he were a get-a-way-with-it jerk man/boy.

"Y'all can't be wandering this town at this time of night. Put him on the couch and talk about it, sweetie."

Jackie hated when Deidre called her sweetie. It was cocksure arrogance and Jackie didn't want any of that...not now. She needed her mother-in-law to be firm, to keep Clarence in line. Deidre failed. She backtracked at times when it came to her boy.

"Who are you putting on the couch mommy?" Their daughter's question surprisingly shook them.

It was as if Hailey, even at her tender age, caught the nuance of the phrase, "put him on the couch."

"Grandma was referring to daddy, not Clarence Jr.; have I got it right?" smiled a knowing Hailey.

Deidre was amazed. She had been clever to protect the child. The reference had backfired in this case...Hailey could see who was acting more the child? Grandma had been read like an open book. It should have stung but in a way Deidre was pleased. She had a granddaughter who was smart - so smart that she could see through the charade that adults perpetrate.

A car horn broke up the reverie of Hailey's cognition.

"That's them now." Jackie ran to the bay window to make certain that her mom and dad had come to their rescue.

Jackie grabbed the bags. To her kids she gave them a look with a "C'mon you all," that got them in line as she lead her troops out the door. Clarence followed them onto the porch.

Jackie hissed, "The kids and I'll be staying with them 'til you get your act together."

Clarence suddenly turned defiant. She had pushed his button. "You're making a big mistake."

"That's rich coming from you. If not for my love of your mama I'd note the biggest mistake I've made in my life." Jackie could sting like a hornet when she needed to.

Jackie swung the door open to discover Vince and Joe frozen in the shadow of the doorway, scared. Joe's arm was still in mid-air as if to knock.

"Fella's you made it!" Clarence was up. Jackie would never make a scene in front of anyone who worked with

Clarence. She would be dutiful, especially in front of these white boys.

"Sorry we're late." Joe wondered why the suitcases?

Vince wondered as well. "Are we interrupting something?"

Clarence jumped on it. "Not at all."

Jackie didn't miss a beat. "Hi guys. I'm Jackie, Clarence's wife and this is Hailey and Clarence, Jr. We're just running out to give grandma and grandpa their bags. They forgot 'em the last time they stayed over." Hailey gave her mother a look, "*oh another charade*" but she dare not challenge the matriarch in front of the strangers.

Vince bought it hook, line and sinker. So did Joe.

Jackie grabbed the bags with children in tow as they moved to greet her Mom and Dad so they would not accidentally blow their charade.

Clarence diverted their attention. "And this is my mother Deidre." Clarence wasn't sure how his mom would react. She would be dutiful or so Clarence prayed. Like Jackie, she was just that. Deidre wasn't about to give them white boys a hint of trouble in the Wilson household. "Y'all have a seat. It'll take a few minutes to warm this food up."

Clarence's wife and children reentered the picture without the bags where they then disappeared with a command that was pure Jackie. "Off to bed kids." She looked at the white boys, "It's late."

"That's why I'm taking the guys out for dinner." Clarence had to do something. He had two women thoroughly pissed at him caught in a tract with no going back and he needed to escape. Clarence knew that in an instant there could be an explosion.

The women knew how their bread was buttered and with a great deal of hidden resentment they played along. However, Deidre was intent on serving the food, "It's 9:30 son, awfully late to be going out for dinner."

But Clarence was just as determined. "That's why we should be out of your way, Mama, so y'all can rest. It's been a long, long day."

"You're right about that." Jackie was sure that, unlike her Hailey, these white boys couldn't read a charade.

Clarence pushed the envelope. He kissed Jackie on the cheek. As every woman knows, the man doesn't get it or doesn't want to. That's stifling. Clarence's wife played the charade only to have the object of her scorn pull a bullshit move of a kiss on the cheek. Even Judas had more class than Clarence when it came to that kiss, or so she steamed. *Oh he's going to get it when he comes.. home.*

If that kiss wasn't enough, the scorned man of the house uttered the coup de grâce, "Don't wait up. I promise to be in by two."

* * *

Well-dressed Negroes pressed forward as they entered the "KITTY KAT CLUB." A midnight blue haze permeated the-black-as-night-sky aura of the club. Small tables aglow in the light of candle centerpieces enveloped coo-some couples pulsing to the heat of the beat.

The boys felt a rush as they and Clarence approached a stage featuring percussionists clicking on marimbas and cowbells. The musicians banged on pitched tumbadoras - one deeply sonorous, the other higher in tone. When you mixed the congas with the recurring ping of a cowbell and the cry of an unbelievable brassy horn section accompanied by melodic blues guitar and piano, the cornucopia of sound entranced and swayed its audience.

The pianist hammered keys of black and ivory from top to bottom and then from bottom back to top. The groove was good. Women sexually sashayed their bodies to the beat as some sauntered through the club attracting bucks filled with lust.

A smooth velvet voice sang words of love in Espanol. The cadence moved from slow to bright. This was a music neither Beriso boy had heard before. It was African-Caribbean notes of pure pleasure permeating the souls who heard it.

From out of nowhere, an entourage of security escorts swarmed the stage as Tony Williams, beckoned by the pianist, stepped from the shadows of a wing to take a bow. The crowd recognized the renowned drummer with enthusiastic applause.

Clarence felt compelled to rush the stage. The club's master of ceremonies stopped him with a hug and a greeting. "Clarence, man I didn't see you. How you been brotha?"

"Russ, you know better than most. My life's a mirror of my soul." They both broke into laughter followed by wide grins.

The smile wavered slightly as Clarence flipped his head back to the boys standing behind him. "I'm on a mission Russ. Meet my disciples, Joe and Vince Beriso."

The MC extended his hand to both boys, which was readily received. "Hey, you guys into afro-music?"

Clarence delivered dry as cork, "No, they came for the food."

The MC chuckled, tickled by his old friend's mirth of humor.

Clarence put his hand on Joe's shoulder. "This one plays a mean set of drums."

"Is that so?" Russ pushed Joe's modesty blush button as the young Beriso lowered his blood filled head. Joe wondered how Clarence could say such a thing to Russ having never witnessed his ability to play. For Clarence such a notion didn't matter since he heard what Russ had not; a voice heartily filled with passion when it came to playing music.

Russ knew his buddy's cue and patted Joe lightly on the shoulder. "You'll have to play something for us."

Joe moved from cocksure to insecure about his passion. "I'm not sure about that."

"Aw c'mon. I'll join you." Clarence's eyes closed the deal.

"Clarence is a gas on the sax." Russ pushed in the hope that magic might materialize in his club that night. Having a white boy on stage was pure entertainment whether the cracker could play or not. Good or bad, Russ won.

Russ seized the moment as the band finished their set. He headed to center stage and announced over the mic, "We have a special treat for you cats, when the music returns." Russ loved to leave the audience hanging for more.

Clarence and the boys found a table. Drinks and soul food consisting of collared greens, black-eyed peas, southern fried chicken, okra with cabbage was ordered by Clarence without the need for a menu. The food came quickly since there was plenty prepared in the kitchen. The boys devoured the food. They were hungry and to their surprise the dishes were tasty.

The return of Russ signaled the end of the break for "The Blue Notes," who duly returned to their respective instruments.

"The Blue Notes are back but with a spice of variety." The cats in the band shot each other a look. They knew what was coming. Russ frequently brought guests up on stage and that was fine. Someone or maybe *some ones* would get a break for a cigarette and another drink on the house and the chance to mingle with the ladies in waiting.

"My good buddy Clarence, a long-time regular of the Kitty-Kat will spice things up a bit with the dulcet tones of a baritone sax accompanied by...

Russ had forgotten Joe's name. "What's your name?"

"Joe."

"Ah yes, Joe...who'll lay that beat down and more."

Joe claimed the drummer's throne twirling the sticks left by The Blue Notes timekeeper who now was making time with a Kitty Kat favorite as he savored her sultry décolletage while sipping on a Crown Royale. Joe's stomach soured as the room turned stone cold. He could see the looks wondering who and why was this whitey on the stage? Even Vince scrunched in his seat anxious that his brother might bomb.

A hush came over the crowd as Clarence opened with an intricate, silky, smooth, satisfying riff as he tossed it to Joe who slashed a beat that hammered the piano man to push the bass to follow.

A skeptical audience became believers as the improvised band of black and white harmonized perfectly as the tinkle of ebony and ivory solo beckoned Joe to complement it.

The young Beriso took the nod with a vengeance blasting his snare with a series of flam strokes followed by a crash of cymbals that lead to a full tom-tom solo that moved to a sizzling buzzing snare roll that reignited the quartet to go full swing. The explosive romp turned in a direction not expected...the flourishing of emotion wafting through a sea of chords that fell gently on the dancers moving in a rhythm that had a life of its own. The crowd was as invested in this moment as was Clarence, Joe and their two new best friends, the musicians who didn't abandon them. The crowd flowed like a school of fish moving in a swarmed unison of silver through a sea of blue notes flying above, below and beyond the hearts that beat within those on the dance floor. The spectators sipping their drinks sensed a life's moment and turned their previous disregard into an embrace to be part of the community as well. Musical clubs allowed any man, no matter what creed or color to be able to see life through a glass like wall, clear, clear glass that invited any reasonable thinking human being to envision how life could be.

A crescendo of cymbals signaled the rousing finale of a flirtatious, some might even call seductive frolic that enveloped participants in musical motion married to the power of sound. A second of nothing rang out when the music stopped followed by an explosion of applause that rained like a storm.

———

"In the name of the greatest people that have ever trod this earth, I draw the line in the dust and toss the gauntlet before the feet of tyranny, and I say segregation now, segregation tomorrow, segregation forever."

George Corley Wallace
45th Governor of Alabama
1963-1967

CHAPTER TWENTY

MISSION ACCOMPLISHED

Clarence, Vince and Joe walked together under a sky filled with a diamond bright fallen star. "Can you imagine that Joe? Tony Williams, your idol in the same club and you get a nod and a wink. Wow!"

Joe, awkward, was unsure of what to say, so he said nothing.

Vince interpreted the silence for what it was, Joe's insecurity, while Clarence saw wisdom in silence when complimented.

Vince threw his arms around Joe, proud to be his bro. He wanted to shift the focus so he asked, "Whose house is that?'

On the other side of a neat row of hedges lay a mansion lit up as bright as the White House at night.

Joe had lowered his eyes when he felt the "wow" in the compliment from a very talented musician. Upon raising his sight he let out a sigh that stretched the "a" in, "Whoaaaaaaaa."

Clarence let the sight sink in for a second and then exhaled, "That is the John H Johnson pad. The man who founded Johnson Publishing."

Vince wondered aloud, "A Swedish family lives in this neighborhood?"

Clarence's smile gleamed with a glint of light from the mansion. "The man that lives in that house isn't Swedish, he's colored."

Vince countered aloud, "No way!"

Clarence's mouth tightened diminishing the smile. "Have either of you ever heard of Ebony or Jet Magazines?" Vince and Joe didn't have a clue as to what Clarence was talking about.

Clarence calmly said, "Okay," while taking a deep breath. "He is one of the richest men in Chicago and it is known, by those in the know, that when Mr. Johnson calls, the Mayor answers. Johnson Publishing was very supportive of King Richard's reign in Chicago and the Daley family knew well enough to show "that nigger" some damn R-E-S-P-E-C-T!"

"So he's a publisher of magazines - sort of a Hugh Hefner, the local Playboy who made good?" Clarence reacted to Vince's inquiry with a question that rattled in his head; why was it so incredible for white guys to understand that wealth was non-discriminating?

The journey continued to entertain and enlighten Clarence of the divide that existed between black and white. It also tickled him as he pointed out one big house after another filled with celebrated people even they recognized, like Ernie Banks, a.k.a "Mister CUB."

"Besides his success as a ball player, he's a superb businessman. He owns a car dealership named appropriately, Ernie Banks Ford."

"Clarence, he's our dad's favorite Cub. And our dad doesn't like colored people." Joe bit his tongue. He should have kept his mouth shut. There was wisdom in silence.

They walked on in silence as the moon's beams cut shadows that decorated their path. Possibly they had walked a tad too far when Clarence realized they had crossed a line of demarcation.   In Chicago, there were lots of "lines of demarcation." It was hard to keep track of them. On one side of the street, you might be fine, but cross that street and be of the wrong color and you might find that your trip had left you with no out and no where to go.

"What's their business here?" The words crackled in the summer's night air.

Clarence was caught off-guard. He turned to see a large black militant of a man in front of a small gathering staring blankly and incredulous at the intrusion.

Quickly. "Hey, it's okay, they're with me," Clarence finished with a smile.

The militant spokesperson seethed, "It's not okay. They don't belong around here. They're not wanted and certainly not loved, so get them the hell out of here, now!"

"We don't want any trouble. We're leaving." Clarence said it, matter-of-fact. He grabbed each boy's arm and turned him to walk away.

Clarence quietly shared with the brothers, "Don't look back, and just keep walking."

About a block away, Joe had enough nerve to ask, "Who were they?"

"Our watchdogs."

* * *

Vince sat behind the wheel with Joe in the shotgun spot. Clarence peered in through the front passenger's open window.

"Are you sure you don't want me to follow you to the expressway?"

Vince, with complete confidence replied, "We'll be alright."

Clarence nodded. He wanted to say it but hesitated...oh hell, he let it rip, "Must have taken a lot for y'all to come down here."

Both boys acknowledged the question with a nod, one nod being a bit slighter than the other, but nods notwithstanding.

"An experience that I won't forget." Joe's sentiment was obvious in his voice and countenance.

Vince was a bit more reluctant or maybe it was reserved. "Yeah...it was...it was smooth till the end. Thanks for protecting us. We're sorry about your reception in our neighborhood."

Vince turned the key. A backfire put a fright in the boys. They instinctively dived to the floorboard of their auto. Clarence laughed at the reaction. "Sounds like you guys need a tune-up." He turned and headed up the walk to his hearth and home.

Vince and Joe sheepishly gathered themselves. They put the Chevy in gear and headed to the safety of their side of the city.

* * *

Clarence tiptoed his way to bed. He didn't want to wake Jackie, for lots of reasons including the one most men can relate to, "the fear of having to talk about it." The feel of the silk sheet on his body encumbered by only his boxers gave Clarence a moment of ecstasy. He made it.

Unexpectedly the sleeping beauty awakened. "Done roustabouting?"

Clarence rolled on his side away from the voice. "You don't get it, do you?"

"Oh I get it? You gambled with our money; money we need for our livelihood, that's what I get." If there was one thing Jackie did get, it was the ability to stay on point.

"I won. So what's your point?"

"You put your family in jeopardy. You ran the streets till what hour and for what?"

"To better our lives Jackie."

"Life was fine, why mix it up with whitey?"

Clarence took a deep breath accompanied by a sigh. "You willing to listen? To learn what's in my heart?"

Jackie was struck by the timbre of her husband's voice. Her silence signaled a willingness to listen.

"The night King died, I got to thinking - how can I do my part to keep his dream alive." Clarence shifted his head. "A flash of light shined on me when them boys entered my life. I knew this was my chance."

Jackie's eyes had a glaze of wonderment; he had enchanted her and she didn't care if it showed. Jackie had deep inside a burning desire for a man who constantly questioned life asking, "Does it get better?" Clarence noticed the shift in Jackie's demeanor. He loved everything about his Eve and wanted to stay with her. He was convinced there was no zenith they couldn't reach. He was that passionate about the love of his life.

Jackie broke the silence. "To do what Clarence – how does life change with your interaction with those boys?"

"To show them the truth." Clarence cracked a wee smile. "Don't you see...those boys have grown up hearing nothing but lies about us... you, me, the lil ones. I saw it tonight. They've only heard that we are lazy, shiftless, thugs and unwilling to work for our supper. Don't you think that's sad?" He stared deep into Jackie's eyes.

"And you plan to change that Clarence?" Jackie penetrated not only the eyes of her man holding her now in his embrace but also his soul.

"I do. And hopefully, they'll take from their experience with me that racism based on ignorance is just wrong." Clarence was sure as rice on rain about that.

Jackie kissed Clarence. A kiss that was holding on to the world and moving on to what was next.

"I'm afraid you're going to get hurt." Jackie quietly shed a sole tear that glistened in the moonlight. It was anything but tiny and had the movement of a wave. Clarence knew he had to slide through a walk of fire. The wrong words at this moment would jam the deal. "C'mon baby, you and Mama got to stop holding me up, which prevents me from being my best. You get it don't you love?"

Jackie held him in her arms.

"Please baby. Let me be a man." Clarence and Jackie's eyes locked on one another.

They held on to each other and by the grace of God, they held on to their world.

———

CHAPTER TWENTY-ONE

BACK TO NORMAL

A hum, a pulse, a buzz erupted in sound surround as heavy traffic and crowds encircled the beautiful friendly confines of Wrigley Field, home of the Chicago Cubs. The electrifying stadium sign ran a ticker of stellar names in baseball: BANKS vs. MAYS. Those two men were the epitome of what it was to be a genuinely gifted ball player.

Inside the ballpark the match ensued with the Giants leading the entire game by a solitary run. It was only in the ninth that the crowd roared excited by two Chicago base runners advancing to second and third but held from scoring as the incomparable Willie Mays made a great play which prevented the Cubs from scoring. The fans were disappointed until they heard the crackle of the public address announcer, Pat Pieper, say the words, "Now batting, number 14, short-stop, Ernie Banks." Wrigley Field denizens roared for their hero known affectionately as "Mr. Cub" to bring those runners home. Banks took a few practice swings and then with amazing grace, he stepped into the box. The entire stadium audience rose to their feet. There was nowhere to go, it was after all the bottom of the ninth with two outs. Ernie Banks would have to take it down, take it all the way down, take it all the way down to victory or defeat.

John, Vince and Joe were fervently praying that Banks would save the day as the cheers resounded.

"Hey dad! Why do you like Ernie Banks so much?" Joe played his line beautifully. Ernie took a ball on the outside corner that was unbelievably called by the ump a strike. John looked perturbed. What kind of question was that to ask at this point in time? "What's not to like about Banks?"

Joe, being a wise ass retorted, "But he's colored, ain't he?"

John miffed with Joe. "He's no nigger, he's a ....he's Mr. Cub. Big difference."

Mr. Cub fouled off the next ball and now there lay only one strike left for a Giants win. But in baseball, that one strike at times can be very elusive. The pitcher took his wind up and delivered a blazing fastball. A crush of wood on ball made everyone jump as Banks annihilated the ball deep, way deep to center field. Willie Mays, the other future baseball Hall-of-Fame candidate, got on his horse and trotted back, way back to the warning track. Mays leaped to catch the ball and it looked as if it was over when a burst of wind off the lake whipped the ball back to bounce in front of Mays. It was freaky but something Wrigley field partisans had seen before. The ball's arc back was enough to distract Mays who somehow remarkably recovered to retrieve the ball and blast it into the cut-off man, who gunned it to the plate only to have the Cub that had been on second slide ever so gingerly under the catcher's tag. The umpire's arms indicating "safe," set off an eruption of Cub fan delight that shook the stadium's rafters. The home team had prevailed. The raising of the white flag with the blue "W" made it official. The Cubs and Mr. Cub in particular had defeated Mays and his Giants in the nick of time.

*

What were the chances? In a large parking lot outside of Wrigley Field following the Cubs win over the Giants, there they were.

Clarence noticed the boys first. "Joe! Vince!"

Joe, Vince and John acknowledged Clarence who had secured his kids in the back seat of his car.

Joe answered on behalf of all, "Clarence?"

Clarence smiled. "I didn't expect to see you guys so soon."

John responded with a query, "Keeping things under control I hope?"

"Dad, Clarence does a great job." Vince defiantly cared less if he got the "stare."

"About time." John's retort was directed more at his son's insolence than it was at Clarence's perceived ineptitude.

Clarence bristled inside but kept his composure. "Was that a great game or what? With two of baseball's greatest."

John liked that. "Yeah, if we don't see them play again against each other, we'll see them together in Cooperstown in the Baseball Hall of Fame."

"I remember the first time I saw Willie play. It was the '54 World Series." Clarence loved to share that with anyone willing to listen.

"C'mon, you're telling me you saw the basket catch?" John's face seemed to distort as much as his words.

"Cross my heart. I saw the catch." The 1954 World Series highlight that Clarence alluded to, had Willie Mays running deep to the center field warning track with his back to the ball smashed off the bat of Vic Wertz. Somehow that ball fell miraculously into Willie's mitt, which he held like a bushel basket in front of his chest. If that wasn't enough, Mays revolved like a spinning top and fired the ball back into the infield to hold runners from scoring. It is without question, one of the all-time great baseball catches in the history of professional baseball.

"How, did a guy like you get a ticket?" John's question reeked of cynicism.

"You mean a colored guy, don't you?" Clarence could be just as blunt.

"That's not what I meant, but you wouldn't believe me anyway, so, yeah, how did a 'colored guy' like you get that ticket." John wasn't about to be bested by a nigger.

Clarence got the irony. "Well, if it makes you feel better, I was a hot-dog vendor."

The lines on John's face relaxed. "That explains it."

Clarence shot back. "I saw the catch. End of story, I win."

The statement seemed ridiculous to both of them. They bust out laughing in unison and together.

"Daddy, you promised ice cream." The screams of Clarence's kids broke up the tête-à-tête of two hard-core Cub fans. Each patriarch left the friendly confines of Wrigley Field feeling good with the win secured by Mr. Cub.

John noticed Clarence's car for the first time. "Nice car! What's it, a '68 Impala?"

"Yep! Got it the moment when the new models came out." Clarence noticed John's eyes widen.

"You don't say?" John's surprise was evident. Nervously John broke the silence. "Baseball. Something we can all relate to, huh?"

Clarence picked up on the shift, "Yeah, I guess so."

"Oh, you might want to fix the broken mirror," John couldn't help pointing out the imperfection which made Vince and Joe uncomfortable knowing that the assholes on their block had caused the damage.

Clarence let the comment go. He knew the Chief's intent and it wasn't worth the effort on what had otherwise been a beautiful day for a ballgame.

* * *

From the kitchen, Gloria carried two tumblers. Upon reaching John in his armchair, she handed him one of the tumblers. "Thought you might like a nightcap."

"Thanks." John gave his gal a look of approval.

John put the paper he had been reading down. Now was their time in the day when they talked as man and wife. Gloria insisted on it and told him that without it, she wasn't interested in giving him what he craved, hot steamy sex.

That insistence caught John's attention. So when the tumblers came out, that's when the paper, radio, TV or any other distraction was put on hold. For two people who wanted to share life as lovers and friends, it was a fait accompli that they must take the time to talk...just talk and share the agony and ecstasy of their lives. How erotic that promised to be and was.

John's initial reaction (which he kept to himself), "Why the hell do we need this?" underwent a metamorphosis as Gloria revealed her feelings about their marriage and why she found her husband amazing. Gloria knew how to balance the bitching with the praise. Sometimes the conversations were as rich as hot steamy sex. It was the aphrodisiac that made the sex that evening even sweeter. That holy grail of passion - sex - made life so complete and yet so fucked up that maybe "just talking" wasn't so bad after all. By the second week of this drill, John was captivated by Gloria's longing for him and the revelation of the many nights she cried herself to sleep worried sick that she might lose her man that night to fire; the hellish hot stereotypical version of hades or the shiny bullet fire that stops a beating heart instantly in the unsafe time of 1968. John grew to thirst and hunger for "just talking" time and became a firm believer that it made their passion and their union richer.

John's only reluctance was "starting" the conversation. Gloria could live with that so she initiated the conversations.

"So, did y'all have fun at the game?" Gloria figured this would be an easy opening, so she could get to the stuff that was really on her mind. Frankly what Gloria was doing for her fireman was as good if not better than therapy. In some ways it was better, since you got to tell your mate how you really felt without a third wheel interpreting your thoughts and feelings. Besides, they couldn't afford a therapist. She repeated it to prompt John to respond. "So, did y'all have fun at the game?" Once the door was opened with the ritual of asking the question twice, John's tongue became untied and he could talk. "Boy oh boy, we sure did. But you'll never guess who we ran into the parking lot?"

Gloria was surprised with her husband's need to go first with his problem. Usually, once the ice was broken he responded with a prompt answer and then allowed Gloria to discuss what was on her mind when it came to "them." Gloria was smart enough to know when to listen, and this was definitely a time for listening. "I can't imagine, who?" Gloria said it with a naughty, smile.

John loved that about her. "That colored guy the boys work for." John saw the puzzled look in Gloria's eyes. "The Clarence fellow."

Gloria had to think twice; who the hell was Clarence? She didn't want to appear stupid. Instead she feigned shock, "Really?"

John went with shock. It wasn't worth a fight and if he played his cards right, the night would end in connubial bliss. So he tread carefully with his reply; he didn't want to upset the evening's later agenda. "I can't put my finger on it, but it was as if the boys were hiding something from me and their foreman was in on it." As soon as John used the word, "foreman," Gloria got it.

"They've been acting strange ever since they got those jobs," spoken in the voice of a mother who made it explicitly clear, that she didn't want her sons working in an all-black factory in the heart of 1968. Never again would she stand for compliant agreement with a husband just because she was "the little woman."

John acted nonchalantly. He wasn't going to let her comment filled with the ghost of, "I told you so," laced through it get to him. "True, but this is different."

"Well, I don't want to upset you, but I saw a colored man drop the boys off yesterday in front of the house."

"When? After work?"

Gloria thought on it for a moment, "Yeah, it was after 5 so I would assume so."

John took a sip from his drink. "Why didn't you mention it when I called from the station last night?"

Gloria merely stared back at her husband. He had every right to be upset. She should have told him.

"Was it Clarence?"

"I've never seen the man, John, so how would I know that?"

"Right." John shuffled. "Did you see the car he was driving?"

"Yes. It looked a lot like yours, just a different color. Why?" Gloria sipped from her drink.

John took a heavy drag off of the cigarette he'd been smoking while having his tumbler of elixir. Yes, there was something to be said for the "just want to talk" sessions. John found out what his wife really felt about their life together. He was a bit unsure of his place with her. He didn't want to lose the heart of his woman; she really was the love of his life. Even when the talks hurt a bit it felt good to know that he could fix things and more importantly, how to do that. But every now and then it was his turn to bitch when he discovered what truly transpired when he was away on a 24-hour-shift. Gloria would make up for her remission. He was certain of that. What he wasn't certain of was what his boys were hiding. That was but a matter of time and John vowed he'd find out that night.

***

John lifted the garage door. He sat behind the wheel of the Bel Aire and pointed a flashlight at the speedometer. John got out. He slammed the door. "Fuck, they lied to me."

John walked back into his house. He moved immediately to the stairs leading to the bedrooms. "Boys, down here now." John made sure they heard him.

"What's wrong John?" Gloria knew the tenor of her husband's voice so well that his distress seemed overwhelming.

When the boys reached the first floor, they were met with a stern face, weathered from fighting infernos. "Where were you two last night?"

"Here," offered Vince.

"Try again."

Joe didn't like where this was going. "Nowhere."

That "nowhere" was it. John struck both sons across the side of the head. The boys fell onto the sofa, covering their heads with the sofa pillows. Gloria grabbed at John's arm, begging him with her eyes to stop.

John, infuriated with their less than forthright response to his question, could only see rage and struck at their pillows.

"Don't lie to me!"

Gloria put herself between John and the boys. "Stop it!"

He already had when he elected to strike at the pillows rather than their heads. He had no intent to hit his wife. That was not something he could ever do. He directed his ire at the boys. "You were with that nigger, weren't you?"

Gloria was now dumbfounded. "What are you talking about?"

John flung a crinkled paper at the boys. The mileage recorded on the log for the car was twenty miles less that what the speedometer showed. The boys had to keep a log of their trips, mandated by the old man. They hated it but it was their father's way of monitoring their driving habits.

"Boys?" It was Gloria's way of getting into the game without committing to too much.

John elicited the charges. "Let's start with sleeping at the ball game. How late were you up? You guys are something. You question my ethics but you guys are good at the art of deception. It must run in the blood. Your mother saw that nigger drop you off after work."

"What's going on?" Now Gloria was invested.

"All right. Yeah, we were out with Clarence." Vince thought it best to get it over with.

"You snuck out?" Mom was amazed at the newfound audacity.

"It's not Vince's fault. He was looking out for me." Joe was keen to help Vince.

"That's it. You two are done with that factory!" John had said it, not Gloria. It now was so.

Vince defied him. "You can't make us quit."

"Wanna bet?" John wasn't having any of it.

Joe joined with his brother. "It's because of you we're in this mess. We know how you got our jobs."

That put an entirely different spin to the issue at hand. John caught by surprise, wanted to kill the subject.

"Jobs are hard to get. We need one so we're not giving up our jobs, or looking for new ones."

"You'll do as I say!" John went to raise his hand and Gloria caught him with a simple, "John!"

The boys jumped up off the couch. Joe jumped in first, "You don't own us. Slavery was abolished with the 13th amendment in 1865."

John scowled at the boys. Gloria shot him a look followed by an appropriate moment of awkward silence.

"I never in a million years would have thought you to be a racist...till now." That "till now" put a dart in John's heart; stunned, he barely noticed Vince exit.

* * *

A small retinue of Anderson employees surrounded Clarence sitting at his desk. He knew why they were there. He reached into his wallet and pulled out what they all wanted to see. "Behold my friends. A receipt for three at the Kitty Kat Club."

"Hey, they were supposed to go to your house." The belt loader said it for all of them.

"They showed. Then we went for dinner at the Kitty Kat Club. We just had to break bread before midnight. It didn't matter where."

"How do we know that receipt is legit?" Someone asked the unthinkable of Clarence, but it was on the minds of every employee in the bet.

"Ask Lucille. She was there. Or call the club. It's hard to miss two white boys in a sea of black people." Clarence thought the latter fact was so obvious but elusive as well. Clarence peered back into the retinue, not sure who asked that question and very sure he really didn't want to know. "Or you could trust that I'm telling you the truth. How novel would that be?"

Reggie grabbed for his wallet. He handed over the money he lost. "I know the MC. So I know the story to be true."

Clarence put a check by his name as he dropped the bet into a cigar box. "Thanks Reggie. Who's next?"

A line of cigar box contributors filed past as they dropped dollars. Clarence checked them off the list one by one.

"Like an unchecked cancer, hate corrodes the personality and eats away its vital unity. Hate destroys a man's sense of values and his objectivity. It causes him to describe the beautiful as ugly and the ugly as beautiful, and to confuse the true with the false and the false with the true."
                                        - Martin Luther King Jr.

CHAPTER TWENTY-TWO

MISUNDERSTANDING

Vince and Joe donned their monkey overalls in the men's bathroom when a toilet flushed as Larry, the shipping clerk, emerged from the stall. With a look of relief on his face, he exhaled, "Amen, amen...ten pounds lighter."

Vince fanned his nose. "Glad someone feels better."

Larry washed his hands and nodded in agreement, acknowledging the boys. "The two aces. Y'all sure made Clarence a lucky man."

Joe didn't quite get his drift. "It was just dinner."

"Dinner?" The shipping clerk grabbed a paper towel to dry his hands. "Well, that dinner made him a fortune. We all bet him that you'd never show." He finished drying his hands and walked out.

The boys both looked at each other in the mirror along the wall. "Damn! That means we were nothing but novelties." Vince said it to Joe as if to remind him of what the old man always said, "Don't ever trust a Moulie..a fucking Moulie...fuck, you know you can't trust 'em."

Joe exhaled a heavy sign followed by words of disappointment, "And I thought we were friends."

Vince put his arm around his brother because he loved him. "Never trust a Moulie. Maybe the old man was right. God bless him, even though at times I hate him."

"What are we going to do Vince? Maybe we should do as dad wants and quit."

"We ain't quitting. Besides I am not eating the old man's crow after telling him he couldn't tell us what to do. We'll figure it out. For now, don't say a word Joe!"

Joe nodded. They needed to stick together at work and also at home. Life was not easy for young men in 1968.

* * *

The earth was spinning towards that Noon hour lunch break.

Walking through the front doors was Lawrence, Faye's son. Lawrence was welcomed by one and all; they always loved Lawrence even if they didn't love Faye. It was Faye who brought it all home. "Baby, whatcha doing here?"

Lawrence answered truthfully but somewhat unintentionally cryptic, "Clarence invited me to come."

Clarence moved to greet Lawrence when Faye whirled, "What's going on Clarence? Why you ask my boy to come down to a factory that can't offer him what he really needs, a job."

Clarence let the invective glide over his back as smooth as a note on a French horn. Clarence took in the room with his eyes. "Can I get everyone's attention...your attention please. The "s" on the pronunciation of "please" stretched for more than a country mile.

The gathering quieted. Clarence put his arm around Lawrence. "For those of you who don't know Lawrence," Clarence smiled at Lawrence, "he graduated high school at the top of his class. He was the valedictorian."

Applause swept through the living, standing, breathing, crowd standing before them. Clarence resumed. "Now before y'all, go off to lunch, all sour about your losses," Clarence took in the room with anticipated pause, "take comfort in knowing you've given Lawrence a shot at a college education."

A "baffling wave" moved over that same crowd, wondering what the hell the foreman was alluding to. Clarence pulled a cigar box from nowhere, the way a magician pulls a rabbit out of a hat. With cigar box in hand, he grabbed an envelope stuffed with money on top of the receptacle that held the wagers. Clarence, tapped the envelope and decreed, "You can thank the church for that portion of the contribution." The word church sounded bigger than life.

Clarence brought the bounty to Faye. She had kept her distance and yet positioned herself close enough to watch Clarence with her young. She too was baffled but then it hit her. The bets and the envelope of money from the church was exactly what her son needed to meet the requirement of unpaid tuition for him to enroll in college. Her eyes overflowed with tears of sheer star-like delight. Her faith was her rock and her prayers somehow were answered. She erupted in Mahalia Jackson fashion. "God bless you Clarence."

Reggie rarely broke ranks first. He questioned Clarence. "You been planning this all along, haven't you boss?"

Clarence beamed the smiling grill of a "53 Buick," known for its rack of teeth, uppers and lowers. "Yep."

The simplicity of that answer ignited most of the co-workers. Joe and Vince's reaction was anything but warm.

Clarence sensed their distaste and immediately recognized them for their contribution. Cleverly he laid more of the negative "flame" of their ignition on Faye than on himself. "Faye, there's someone else you might want to thank. Had they not gone on an adventure, and moved outside of their world into ours, if only for a night, that cigar box would be light, and devoid of a contribution from me, too busy paying off all the debt I'd have owed all the employees who bet against hope."

Clarence shined a spotlight on the young white men and waited for Faye to make a move. Faye approached the brothers cautiously. Vince and Joe instinctively pulled away. Faye played on their fear immobilizing them momentarily as she grabbed-hugged them.

A big squeeze later, Faye set them free. "Thank you, thank you, thank you Vince and Joe." That was the first time Faye had acknowledged them by name. "You have no idea how important this is to Lawrence and to me. It affects our lives. It makes life worth living. All I can say to Clarence and each of you is thank you for giving that to us."

A window slammed open. Dane looked down at the gathering from his perch in the sky. Everyone waited to hear Zeus. "Clarence?"

Clarence looked back at Zeus. He caught his eye.

"The Chief gave us a good report! Our production last Saturday met Field's deadline and we've now got their business!"

Like Moses chosen ones who dined on manna, everyone on the floor fed on those words. A good report meant no shutdown of the plant, no loss of work, no layoffs. Hearts held out amongst friends on the floor with renewed hope that God would bless them with continuous work.

So for a moment all was perfect.

Co-workers began to pat the whiteys on the back. Even the two troublemakers who engineered the oil spill respectfully paid homage to the brothers.

"You know what would cap this off?" Clarence had their attention. "A juicy beef from Gina's."

Reggie asked, "Sounds good. Vince and Joe, will you do us another run?"

Clarence upset that Reggie interrupted his timing was terse in his reply. "Who said anything about a run?"

Reggie shook his head. "Then, What?"

The unthinkable was heard. " We all go to Gina's." Clarence was fearless. "All of us, now!"

The vat loader couldn't fathom it. "Are you kidding? There's a dozen of them hoods down there."

The workers lost heart - it was noticeable in their faces.

Clarence turned them. "There's more of us than there are of them."

Reggie felt the "us." "Yeah, c'mon, I'm sick of us being cowards. I'm with Clarence."

When a flock is lost, there are no heights in life. Clarence challenged them. "I don't know about y'all, but I'm not about to let Martin's death go in vain. I'm going to lunch."

Clarence walked out of the factory by his lonesome self. But as he walked he picked up disciples. Reggie was on his right; he voiced a concern, "I'm broke." To his surprise Clarence found walking on his left, Dane who proclaimed, "Not a worry. I'm buying. Lucille's going to hold down the fort, but don't let me forget to get her a beef as well."

* * *

Like an army on the move, they, Anderson and Company, literally, headed for Gina's. To everyone's surprise they were able to walk under the viaduct and enter Gina's as easy as any white person.

As they entered, the clink and decibel hum of a bustling restaurant dimmed.

Serving a busy counter of customers, Gina had hardly noticed the arrival of the new clientele. Clarence's voice caught her attention. "Hey stranger!"

Gina gasped. "Clarence?" Gina didn't hesitate to come out from the counter and welcome her long lost friend with a hug. A few customers grabbed their sandwiches and headed for the exit. Gina and Clarence noticed the departures.

"Not to worry, they'll be back, or maybe they won't. Make yourselves comfy." With the white flight, more than enough seats opened up for all to find a place.

Clarence and Dane took two seats next to each other at the counter. Gina attended to them first. "What it'll be, boys?"

"Beefs and a cold one for everyone. My tab."

"Wow Dane, can't get enough?" Gina smiled devilishly at Anderson.

"Guilty as charged. I love your sauce!" Now it was Dane's turn to talk naughty.

"So, where you been Clarence? You were one of my best regulars. Where'd you go?" Gina seemed to be oblivious to the gangsters on her doorstep or perhaps she didn't care. She had her shotgun.

Enough talk. Gina had work to do. She served up the beefs and drinks quickly. These new customers deserved her attention.

* * *

Having delivered their beefs and cold ones, Gina tendered a check to Dane. She spoke to Clarence. "Well, I'm glad you're back. I know Jimmy would be if he was here."

Clarence's eyes dropped. "I'm sorry about Jimmy." Clarence paused, "I guess it's been a long time."

Gina took the cash from Dane who added, "I need one to go for my secretary. I forgot to have you put that on the bill, how much more do I owe?" Gina counted the money and with a swirl popped it into the cash register. " Don't worry about that Dane, it'll be on me, my treat." Gina headed to the kitchen to make one more.

As Gina returned with the extra beef, the Watchdogs appeared, two with baseball bats in hand. "What're you niggers doing in here?" It was the head punk that hung under the viaduct with a colleague who reiterated the sentiment, "You know the rules."

Clarence calmly looked at the array of white punks standing beside and behind their spokesperson. He wasn't afraid to say it. "Rules say it's a free country."

One of the punks shoved Clarence. "Shut your mouth nigger!"

Clarence fell back into the arms of his co-workers. Reggie reacted and shoved the punk who touched Clarence all the way back to the head goon. Jostling broke out. The two punks with bats began to lift their clubs until gunfire erupted. Every soul, no matter the color, froze trying to assess, "Who the hell was carrying heat?"

The moment was broken by the shrill of an angry female voice. "What the hell are you doing in my place?" Gina's eyes were on fire as she looked at the leader of the Watchdogs.

A white voice answered the question, but it wasn't a punk, it was Joe. "Those punks want us out."
The head punk studied the boys. He locked onto Vince and Joe's eyes. He experienced an epiphany. "Are you the beef boys?"
Another punk affirmed his righteousness, "I told you - I knew it... they're nigger lovers.
Gina hissed. "Hey, read the sign!   This is my restaurant!
Silence. A staring match ensued.
Drawing her gun down from an upward position to a foregone conclusion, Gina shouted, "Get out or you'll get a taste of buckshot."
Silence.
The punks noticed the torn up ceiling and with that they began to slither out. From within a mass of heads floating toward the exit came a song out of key, "This ain't over."

* * *

John paced on the firehouse floor. Shaken. Upset. He gazed out the window looking for light. His eyes shifted to Charlie's who sat on the hood of the Chief's car. "I'd like to clock that Clarence right in the kisser."
Charlie, in an undertone, "What would that solve Chief?"
John shot Charlie a what-the-fuck look. In self-doubt John cried out, "How could my boys defy me? Their whole lives have been my whole life! I've tried to protect them." A deep, bitter toned exhale followed, "Now they despise me."
The sidekick didn't waver in propping up a man among men. "Aw, Chief, the boys adore you. Don't you know that? They're just trying to form their own opinion about the world,

make their own way. Were you any different when you were their age?"

John shook his aching head side-to-side. "Calling me a racist. I know what a racist is when I see one and I am no racist. Yeah, I have a dim view of coloreds, niggers, moulie's, but a lot of people have a dim view of wops...guineas like me. The blacks that are responsible like Ernie Banks get my vote. Why's that racist?"

"Chief, was Patrick a racist when he called you a dago at Gina's?" John wondered, how did he do it? Red was more than just a wheelman; he was part psychologist. John's glance at Charlie said it all. Charlie nailed it and John was suddenly ashamed as he plopped into a chair.

For whatever it was worth, Charlie was a man's marine. Semper Fi! He wasn't about to leave a good man behind. "Look Chief, times are changing. If you don't adapt, you're going to find yourself in the minority. And that's your call, buttttt," Charlie's head revolved with the thrill of the "t" to denote justification, "it could affect your relationship with your sons."

"That's what I'm afraid of." A deep sigh of relief helped bring his blood pressure down. At least now he had a clue, but still he sought Charlie's counsel. "So, what do I do?"

"For now let them go. Or they'll let you go. Give it time, it'll all work out. You'll see."

* * *

As the punks exited Gina's, a beer keg delivery truck pulled up and parked parallel to the doorway. The driver exited the truck. He noticed the caravan of young slick-backed-hair-men crossing the street. He grabbed his clipboard as he closed the door to the cab of his truck.

Upon entry, the deliveryman questioned if he had the right place. The restaurant was filled with niggers. Where were all the white people?

"What's new, Paulie?" Gina caught the look of confusion on the face of her visitor.

"Same old, same old, Gina, which is more than I can say for this place."

"You mind your business and I'll mind mine. Which as you can see is pretty good right now. Every table's filled." Gina wasn't taking shit from her deliveryman. She was after all, the fuckin' customer. Gina took the clipboard from Paulie's hand and signed receipt of his delivery.

Clarence and Dane clinked their glasses toasting themselves to a second glass of beer. Dane was in a rare happy mood. Clarence had transformed his work force and profits were up. Dane may have been a capitalist at heart but he was touched that his employees came together for the young man's college, even if it required Clarence's slight of hand. Dane pledged to himself that he would write a check also to help the kid. Clarence had been good for Dane, and Dane wanted to be good for a good man.

"A toast to Anderson, Inc. We live another day." Dane celebrated by holding his glass mountain high.

"And many more." Clarence knew his fate was tied to that of Dane's and Anderson, Inc. So he wanted many more toasts to a successful partnership; his labor and loyalty for a livable wage. The clink of their glasses solidified the deal. To some that might not seem much, but to Clarence, it was as good as it got for most men of color in 1968.

* * *

The punks chuckled as they siphoned gas from the delivery truck's tank into empty beer bottles that they topped off with wicks made of ripped cloth from their shirts. Gas overflowed from the siphon and spread underneath the truck.

* * *

Dane swirled what was left of his beer in his glass the way one twirls a glass of wine to sniff the aroma and the tannins of the grape. A confession was on the horizon. "I know I made your life a hell when I made you hire the Beriso boys."

"Made me hire?" Clarence stressed the "me."

"Touché. I hired them but I had to do what I had to do to keep all of us in jobs, mine included. I needed the Chief's help with the inspectors and all their damn infractions. The fines would have killed me. The boys were the quid-pro-quo. My hands were tied."

"And you have a safer plant, correct?" Clarence knew the answer.

"Yes, it's safer, which makes me a better man, but it came at a bad time when I could least afford it."

"Not when it comes to safety."

"You're right." Dane connected with Clarence. "No hard feelings Clarence?"

"Not at all sir."

"Dane...it's Dane. No more sir shit."

Clarence was pleased and he beamed brightly as the restaurant lit up like a Christmas tree on fire.

———

"War, huh, yeah
What is it good for
Absolutely nothing"
-Edwin Starr

WAR
Written by Barrett Strong, & Norman J. Whitfield.
Published by:
Lyrics © SGiaony/ATV Music Publishing LLC

CHAPTER TWENTY-THREE
THE LAST BATTLE

The punks busted into hyena laughter as their Molotov missiles sailed through the diner's front windows. Glass shattered in every direction raining on customers sitting in the booths by the windows. Customers used their pitchers of beer to drown the wicks on fire to prevent an explosion.

But an elusive Molotov ignited lighting in the front door hallway.

Gina burst out of the kitchen as she heard the crowd's panic to get out of the restaurant. Another Molotov flew in and lost its wick in flight. The bottle busted up on the floor and that gas and wick ignited together causing a fire on the tile floor. Gina grabbed two wet towels and smothered the fire. Clarence found a fire extinguisher and battled to rid the entrance of flames. It was the entrance and the exit and key to their escape.

Another flaming Molotov hit window debris and spun in the air. The forklift driver miraculously caught it the way a receiver comes up with an impossible catch in the corner of an end zone while still getting two feet inside the lines. Just as quickly as he grabbed it he tossed it back and this time it landed under the beer truck. The back end of the truck erupted. Paulie, just about to start the engine, jumped out of the cab and ran from the flash. It was only moments later that the gas tank exploded.

The explosion sucked all of the air out of Gina's diner knocking and sending people airborne. Insanity broke out as clothes caught fire. Fortunately co-workers frantically swatted out flames.

Fire departed and smoke arrived. Smoke was a killer.

Everyone wanted out. The blistering heat from the burning delivery truck made it tough to breathe.

Gina immediately flipped on every exhaust fan in the kitchen area - opening up the airflow in the diner. Grandma had grabbed the little ones and shooed them into a bathroom. She wet dishtowels and had the boy and girl follow her example. They held the wet towels up to their nose and mouth.

Gina grabbed the phone and thanked God that there was a dial tone followed by an operator who promised to send help.

If a burning truck weren't enough, fire coated kegs of beer flew off the delivery truck flying toward the diner. One keg crashed through the door and came within inches of maiming Clarence who was using the extinguisher to put out flames blocking their egress.

Faye helped her son Lawrence off the floor. The shock wave from the gas tank exploding disoriented him. A look of terror filled their faces. Lawrence could see Mama's lips moving but he couldn't hear her.

To protect themselves from flying deadly objects, co-workers overturned tables, stacking them to build a shield from the explosive kegs.

Vince and Joe disseminated as many wet towels as they could whip up. Faye with Lawrence's help aided the injured.

Sirens penetrated the inferno. The calvary was on the way. God granted them hope, the most powerful aphrodisiac known to man.

* * *

When the call came in, the Chief and Charlie were on an inspection and not at the district station. Both were shocked by the alarm. Firemen respond to impersonal calls all day. It's a tough job and sometimes it hurts to pull a lost soul out of a building in a body bag, but it's impersonal. Gina's was personal. Both men treasured the joy of Gina, the joy of the eatery.

John remembered that he had made both boys a lunch before he left home to report for work. That helped an erratic stomach for a moment, until John saw in his mind, restaurant regulars, people he knew, burning to death.

With wet towels over their head that Clarence demanded they wear, Vince and Joe dashed out to their right, away from the delivery truck. They saw the first truck arrive on the scene. The men on the truck recognized the boys and the radio crackled, "the Chief's boys are out and okay." Charlie stepped on it, flying down Grand Avenue and ignoring red traffic lights.

The engineer on board the truck held rank and ordered a line on that front entrance immediately. Within 35 seconds a line of water poured coolness and air into the restaurant and made it possible for the inhabitants to escape. They still had to fear the eruptions of the beer truck and the possibility of more flying kegs barreling off of its shelves. But somehow, miraculously they all got out with Clarence dead last. He took three steps towards the opening of the underpass and collapsed.

The Chief's car arrived. John and Charlie stepped out of it into a crowd lured by the magnetism of a fire. As he moved forward he saw his boys, roped out by the police, crying out for "Clarence."

Clarence was lying on the ground with two fire fighters, over him. John rushed up. "What's the status on this guy."

"Smoke inhalation," coughed up an Irish red headed fire fighter.

"You try to resuscitate him?" John was waiting for affirmation.

An Irish fireman with a heavy brogue lilted a, "No. I'm not comfortable putting my lips on a nigger, sir."

John shoved both men aside as he dropped to his knees and immediately did what the Irishmen failed to do. John pinched the nose and locked lips on Clarence and breathed deeply into him. He then pushed cardiac style against his chest. John did it again and again and again. The roped-off crowd watched in reverent silence. Finally, a gag, a choke and a spurt of foam spewed from the mouth of Clarence.

The bystanders cheered and a couple embraced in a passionate kiss as Clarence regained breath and life.

John fell to his ass and wiped the foamy drool off his lips. The first face he saw that projected "a job well done," was Charlie. John's eyes then caught Clarence's. He turned away from them.

A blaring ambulance ride whisked Clarence out of a neighborhood of hate to a hospital where love was dispensed regardless of color.

* * *

Jackie, Deidre, Hailey and Junior ran down a hallway filled with florescent light. The spectrum was whiter than it was green. In a fortuneteller's world, the hallway was more of a tunnel and the white light was bright and intense beckoning one step into the beyond. Any way you put it, that light was antiseptically uncomfortable.

Room 333 was to their left. The door swung open and, in a flash, Junior and Hailey were on their dad's bed wondering why he had to have tubes up his nose, a big bandage on his head and a head wrap.

Their curiousness was left unanswered by Jackie. "Kids get down. Give your father a break."

Clarence loved having the kids next to him. He had gone to work that day without hugging them before he left home. He vowed he would never make that mistake again...life was tentative.

Deidre, grateful to see her son alive, thanked the Lord. Only then did she brake into a smile.

Jackie wept.

"Aw, c'mon, honey, don't cry." Clarence motioned with a slight nod of his eyes his concern for the kids. He pulled on her hand and brought her in over him for a kiss.

"Oh my God Clarence, I was so scared we'd lost you."

"But I'm here, baby. I'm not going anywhere. I'm with the ones I love." He squeezed her hand for another kiss and then announced proudly, "Gave Lawrence the money for school."

"The Rev. raised all of it?" Jackie was impressed.

"Half."

"What does Lawrence plan to do about getting the rest?"

"He doesn't. The bet came in. I covered it."

"That gamblin' is devil's work. I've told you that son, time and time again, but no matter, I'm proud of what you done for Lawrence." Deidre beamed. Her son was the man she had hoped for. He was a hero.

Jackie echoed the sentiment. "Me too, baby."

Hailey didn't want to be left out and surprised everyone with a declaration, "Junior and I are proud of you too daddy." She hadn't checked with Junior, but she was pretty sure he'd go with her story, which he did. Clarence was impressed by his daughter's ability to think on her feet.

At the door were two familiar faces. Vince and Joe gave Clarence a thumbs-up. He returned the gesture. Clarence pulled his kids closer as he kissed Jackie again. He had an epiphany; he would never take his family for granted again.

The mood abruptly changed as Chief John Beriso arrived dressed in a cleanly pressed full dress blues uniform. He was devoid of the smell of smoke. He had obviously washed it off. John stared at Clarence for a beat. Suddenly he remembered what his mission was. John dug into a bag he carried and pulled out a plaque that read, "On behalf of the city." He handed the plaque to Clarence. He lowered his eyebrow, "For your heroics in saving the lives of fellow Chicagoans, including my sons."

Clarence took a deep breath as he grasped the gravity of the plaque with his name etched in brass. "Wow, this is something!" He smiled proudly.

John felt the pride and for the first time in his life, he empathized with a colored man; make that a man, a proud, proud, busting self-righteous son of a bitch who could not win for losing, "I'm damned if I do and damned if I don't. So I might as well do whatever I want."

John was unsure of how to follow. "For what it's worth."

Clarence's smile stopped John. "We're now even."

At the door stood a mob of reporters and photographers who hurried inside making lots of noise as flashes popped white light strobe trips around the sun. "Chief, explain the investigation?" Another voice queried, "This...in anyway connected to the recent hate crimes near that location?"

John was feeling way off the straight and narrow and didn't want to have to answer because he knew he'd just disappoint them. "Them" was the politicos that he had to kiss to keep his stature as a Battalion Chief.

"Is it true Chief that you suspended members of your company?" asked one reporter.

John looked only at Clarence. "See, ya around. Get well soon Mr. Wilson." He ignored the reporters as he turned to exit through them.

"Chief, how does it feel to be called a hero?"

Clarence got John to look back at him when he let out the cry, "Chief! Thanks."

John nodded and headed toward the exit when the sight of Vince putting his hands through the hair of Lucille and kissing the mulatto stunned him.

Joe got caught in the middle of looks from sibling and father. He looked at Vince and Lucille; he peered at his father; Joe exhibited worry. However, Vince was anything but worried. For the first time in his life the oldest son didn't give a shit what his old man thought. He completed the kiss.

* * *

A parade of Anderson co-workers chanted, "we shall overcome," over and over as they stepped in unison towards the viaduct with kerosene soaked torches for light and protection along with buckets of white wash in hand.

The torches revealed epithets emblazoned on the viaduct brickwork. The bucket holders splashed paint, washing the stains of bigotry from the walls of the infamous demarcation viaduct. The noose of rope that hanged from the structure was burned "in effigy," literally.

After the funeral to eradicate the Watchdogs influence, the faithful met to celebrate life by gobbling mouth-watering beefs previously denied, which made them ever so sweeter.

* * *

John drove from the hospital to home as Joe and Vince stared and locked on him like a deer in headlights. John was too ashamed to return the visual communication. His focus was on the road ahead. "You boys have grown. I, on the other hand, have some growing to do. Times have changed. It's easier to keep it locked inside but the fact is that I don't want to lose my sons. I love you boys and I pray to God you love me." The boys said nothing. They had never witnessed this side of their father before. It had been a long day. John had been relieved of duty due to his sons being victims of the fire. Upon arrival at their home, John, misty-eyed, looked at Vince and Joe in the twilight of the sky. Both sons embraced their father as their mom looked on, happy that her men were safe and at peace with one another.

* * *

Epilogue

Six Months Later

They entered the viaduct laughing. Black factory workers from Anderson were ethereal as they headed without concern to Gina's. Voices rang out, "The judge showed them punks no mercy." "The Watchdogs have been impounded."

"Gina's" had a whole new look with the remodeling that followed an inferno that came to be called, the great *Chicago Fire Under the Viaduct*. There were now two doors of entry and exit, both at the front of the structure separated by the width of the restaurant.

Inside Gina's, patrons, black, brown and white enjoyed their beefs, most with jardinière but some with sweet peppers.

Reggie sat at the counter next to his newfound hero, the Chief, who had to his right his Irish consigliore, Charlie.

Inside the restaurant was a banner that read, "Grand Opening - We're Back!" Captain Patrick O'Malley, now engaged to Gina was working the room greeting every patron on behalf of his fiancé'. He made a point of spending time with Dane. O'Malley knew who was who and like a politician thought it best to get to know the man who owned Anderson, Inc.

Upon Clarence's arrival, Gina gave the foreman a hug and a toothy smile. She then followed with a salutary exclamation inquiry, " Clarence, how the hell are you?"

"I'm fine. I dreamed about you, so that's how much I missed you!" Clarence told it like it was. "But that's one we'll keep to ourselves, okay?" His eyes sparkled with a glint that understated the importance of discretion and accomplishment.

John asked Charlie, "Move one over will you?"

Charlie immediately complied leaving a seat next to John open.

"Chief, how's it hanging?" Clarence busted into a devilish grin.

The Chief snickered. "Not sure I'm willing to share that but if you're asking how am I? I'm fine. Sit down."

Clarence took the open seat. "And the boys?"

"They're wiser than their ages, thanks in part to you. So am I." They both acknowledged each other with a look to what could be. "They've asked about you. They're getting ready for finals and as it turns out, Joe doesn't need to worry about college English. He shocked us all, including his big brother by scoring an all-time high of 5 out of 5 on that advanced placement exam he fretted about. Vince only got a 3, the minimum to pass, but nevertheless you can imagine the kid made his big brother eat a bit of crow."

Clarence couldn't help but laugh. He appreciated the rivalry that existed between the Beriso brothers.

John joined in the laughter. "Who knows, after he gets that drumming craze out of his system, he may prove to be a writer someday."

"Yeah, possibly he can be both a great drummer and a writer…after all he's got talent."

The Chief pondered that thought for a moment and then smiled. "As long as he's happy, I guess that's all that matters."

Clarence extended his hand for a shake. "Congratulations Chief on your promotion."

"It's Division Marshal to you."   Clarence blinked and then realized that John was just pulling his chain. Beriso was decked in the uniform of a Division Marshall, a new responsibility that required supervision of all the men and the Battalion Chiefs of Division District 2. John returned the handshake and smiled, "but let's dispense with rank and keep it simple.   John is what my friends call me."   Clarence appreciated the inference.

"Gina, let's pour Clarence an Old-Style on me." John turned toward Clarence. "I'd join you, but I'm on duty."

Gina poured Clarence a cold one.

Charlie moved with his boss after the promotion, in part out of loyalty to Beriso but also for the substantial raise he received.   He was now more than just a driver; he was the attaché to the Division Commander. "You sure he drinks Old-Style Chief?"

Only Red could continue to call his boss, "Chief," for everyone else, it was Division Marshall.

"He's a Cubs fan - of course he drinks Old-Style!"

Clarence didn't bother to reveal whether he drank beer or not. He grabbed the frosty mug and downed the glass.

John watched Clarence enjoy the beer. He then posed the eternal question that all Cubbies ask, no matter their color or creed. "So what do you think? Is this the year they win it all?"

At that very moment the jukebox blared Chuck Berry's, "You can never tell."   Both men enjoyed the irony of the moment.

***

As it turned out, 1969 would be a banner year for the Cubs only to disappoint in September, the last month of the season. Chicago frittered away an eight game lead to the second place, miracle N.Y. Mets who eventually went on to beat the Orioles in the World Series that year.

Tried-and-true fans, like John and Clarence, were anything but discouraged by the saga of Wrigleyville. When it came to their lovable losers, Chicago fans were eternal optimists who were often heard to say, "Wait 'till next year!"

———